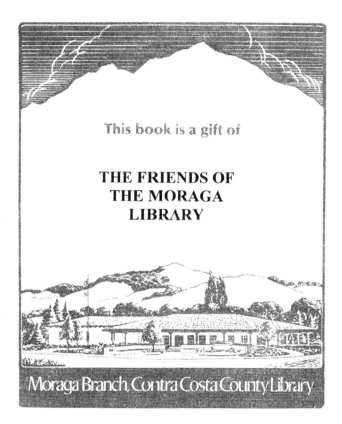

All the Stars in the Sky

The Santa Fe Trail Diary of Florrie Mack Ryder

BY MEGAN MCDONALD

Scholastic Inc. New York

Arrow Rock, Missouri
1848

June 1, 1848, Arrow Rock, Missouri

Jem says why would I be writing in my diary when I could be whittling a whistle out of willow wood. My little brother's all noise. He says, "Florrie, you should be looking at the world instead of some page." This *is* how I look at the world.

Take Arrow Rock. Now that we're leaving for New Mexico Territory, this town is just a story to me. And if you came near for any reason, you'd hear that story, too. It goes like this:

Two men were fighting over an Indian chief's daughter. The chief said whosoever could shoot an arrow the farthest would marry her. One arrow never left the bow. Tell you why. The other man swam out to a sandbar plunk in the middle of the Missouri River. He stood on that sandbar and shot the arrow so's it sailed right across the water and through the sky and over the trees and there was nothing stopping it but a mountain of a stone boulder.

That arrow stuck there, and poof, now there's a

tiny town, where I live, under the scar in the heart of a giant rock.

Lived, I should say. Soon we'll be on our way, where home is out there with the prairie dogs. Nothing but a wagon and all the stars in the sky.

June 2, starting out

Our wagon's loaded to the gills with most things we'll be needing for making a home when we get to Santa Fe, and a few we just plain could not part with. What a tangle! Barrels and ropes and cooking pots, blankets and lanterns and sacks and sacks of foodstuffs, tabletops and bedposts — even Mama's rosewood rocking chair tied to the back. One trunk holds all the medicines, a bottle of matches, and clean clothes we're saving for when we get to New Mexico, including hair ribbons for me and a comb Papa gave Mama before he died.

Mama could not let go of some of Papa's shirts, his Bible, a hat, his knife, or even his medical bag from when he was in the army, so she packed them in a small leather trunk and would not hear otherwise from Mr. Ryder, who is to be our father now that Mama has married again.

I am relieved Mama stood her ground, but I am sadder to leave behind Aunt Florence (my father's sister — I'm named after her) and Uncle Henry than all the belongings in the world. I can't bear the parting — already had three teary good-byes with my dear friend Caroline.

The rest of our things we had to sell. Even my Sunday shoes! I went to pack them in a trunk when Aunt Florence stopped me. She took my shoes, saying, "No pair of shoes in the whole of Missouri's gonna fit by the time you get to New Mexico. You'll be walkin' a whole new path by then."

I fail to see how traveling to New Mexico is going to make my feet so much bigger! But it seemed mighty important to Aunt Florence, so I promised her I would keep it in mind.

One thing nobody knows, but I can tell you, Diary, is that I've hidden something in the barrel of cornmeal with Mama's china dishes. I cannot write it now — Jem keeps lurking around pretending not to be peeking over my shoulder!

June 3, halfway to Independence

Our dog, Mr. Biscuit, seems happier than anyone to be on the trail.

Mr. Ryder saw me scribbling away and says I ought to be putting things down not just for myself but for posterity. I didn't have a single idea what he meant. But then he did explain he was talking about me writing things down for history and all time.

So I'm putting down for all time how Mr. Biscuit got his name. See, Mama makes the best biscuits in Missouri, and once when we were all awaiting to eat a fresh batch, Mama turned her back and our dog did snap up and eat a whole plate full of her biscuits, leaving none for us. Not a one! Ever since, he's been Mr. Biscuit. Before that he was just plain Shep.

The day before we left Arrow Rock, when Mama announced we were leaving Mr. Biscuit behind with the McAlisters, Jem sagged like an old shirt hung to dry. Mr. Biscuit looked at me with such sad hound dog eyes, it near broke my heart. I myself announced that if Mr. Biscuit could not go on the journey, neither would I!

Mama declared she did not know where I got such a stubborn streak. Then Mr. Ryder stepped in and took up the cause for bringing Mr. B with us. He convinced Mama that a dog makes a good watch for the tent door. So here we are.

Poor dog! He was nearly white with light brown spots when we started, but now he is so dusty, he is mostly brown spots!

Later

Now that Jem is nowhere about, I can tell my secret. Directly before leaving, Aunt Florence handed me a jar of honey. Sweet, clear honey, so golden that when she held it up to the light, it glowed amber like a lantern. "Try to make it last" were her final words to me.

The way I figure, if it's *hidden* and I'm the only one knows about it, it'll last much longer. After all, that honey from home will have to last me all the way to New Mexico Territory.

June 4

Mama says we're Ryders now.

Me, I just can't help thinking of myself as Florrie Mack. Always have, always will. A new name pinches me worse than Sunday shoes.

Odd to try to call Mr. Ryder *Papa* now, when in

actuality he is not my real father. Feels strange and forced every time I try. I can say here that my own Papa died when I was still a wee thing and Jem only knee-high to a mosquito. I have little memory of him myself, while Jem has none, and Mama is closed-mouthed on the subject of his death. What I know is that he was an army surgeon in the Mexican War, killed in battle. It gives me some tiny happiness to imagine him saving lives of the wounded.

Mama keeps a picture of him inside the Bible. I have a faint remembrance of sitting on her lap in a dim room with curtains drawn when she sang to me and showed me the sturdy man that was my father. He had long dark hair, nearly always falling over his eyes, Mama said — eyes with laughing lines around them like crow's feet.

I can't truly say I miss my father, gone so long. But I do miss the idea of him.

Mr. Ryder seems a good man most of the time. I'm trying to give him a chance, like Mama asked. He can even be jolly when his mind's not all business — trading, the trip, the trail. Should do Mama good to have somebody nearby with such a cheerful countenance. She's been sad so long, and hasn't ever been keen on making this trip.

Were it not for Mr. Ryder being a trader, we would not be on this journey! He's part-owner of a general store in Santa Fe, where we're headed, which he says is quite the trading capital.

Here goes a list of things I like about Mr. Ryder so far:

He rides a horse well and fast.
He has red hair.
He tells good stories, especially ones about giants.
He shows Jem how to fish and whittle.
He teaches me words in Spanish, like *hola, adiós,* and
    ¿Qué pasa?
He sings in spite of sounding like a crow.
He does not call me Florence.

Things I dislike:

He is not my true father.

Later

I miss Caroline as much as I miss my own name! Will I ever have a friend so dear and sweet? It's lonely out here listening to the whispering of all this grass. If only one of those whispers was a secret told to me by Caroline.

We've heard of hundreds of families heading west for Oregon. They even travel part of the same trail that we do. But Mr. Ryder says I most likely won't meet any other girls, since the Santa Fe is not really for families. It's the route for traders — men like Mr. Ryder who are taking their wares to New Mexico and beyond to sell their goods.

If this route is not for families, I dare say, why ever has he brought us here? I don't think I can stand not having a friend for this months-long journey.

June 5, Independence, Missouri

What a place! Never have I laid eyes on a real and actual city. The hustle-bustle! Noise in all directions. Excitement hangs in the air.

Thousands of oxen and mules graze in the fields, waiting, like us. I'm writing fast as I can so as not to miss one single thing. In the square, Mr. Ryder and many of the traders are packing boxes and bales, laying in stores for the long journey. Mexican traders in their wide-brimmed hats and bright *sarapes* are loading up, calling out *buenos días* and *¿Qué pasa?*

Families bound for the Oregon and California Trails are readying themselves every which way.

I have just seen the town courthouse, which they say looks like Philadelphia's own Independence Hall. And Mr. Ryder has pointed to a hotel where he himself actually stayed the night! He calls it Uncle Wood's Hotel and told Mama and me that it has enough beds to sleep four hundred people!

How I should like to try sleeping on a fancy hotel feather bed. Mama says only, "Watch that your head doesn't swell too big thinking of feather beds. It'll be some long time until we see a bed again."

To think! This is only the beginning.

Late morning

Full half a day it has taken us to be ready to leave. Mr. Ryder has given Jem his own job. A pitcher of grease hangs under the wagon, and Jem's job is to see that the wheels turn smooth. Jem is puffed up as a rooster with his own importance.

I stepped right up to Mr. Ryder, hoping to be told my own duties. He gave me that look. Oh how it sets my blood to boil. I know I'll have to help Mama with the cooking and such, but why is that all I should get to do?

I stood up taller. Mr. Ryder looked around this way and that, then announced that I am to feed and brush the riding horses, Velvet and Rosie.

I could have kissed him on his red face!

later

With a snap of the whip, we're on our way out of town. Finally moving. Every window sash is raised, and the faces of strangers watch our leaving. Do they wish they were going, too?

Mr. Ryder has met up with a short, stocky man they call Frenchie. He's to be head driver in addition to Mr. R. He stinks to high heaven of tobacco! Even so, I can't help but like him. The man sings to the mules in French!

Mr. R. told Mama he's quite reliable, despite the stench. They've traveled this route together any number of times. Frenchie will be in charge of the other wagons, the ones with all the trade goods, from calico cloth, tobacco, vinegar, and carpets to ox yokes and wagon covers. Also the teamsters, mules, and oxen, which Jem says number one hundred. (I doubt he actually counted them.)

We have *uno, dos, tres, cuatro, cinco, seis* wagons

besides our own loaded with goods to trade, more money than I ever heard of! I can see the worry lines crease Mama's forehead, adding it all up. One wagon costs $90, and four yoke of oxen, $200. With the other traders, we are altogether thirty-two wagons!

Midday rest

I dare say we're in Kansas! K-A-N-S-A-S!

So far, there's not a tree, bush, or shrub in sight save for one elm, which stands like a lone soldier on a mound guarding a small creek. That all-alone tree makes me miss Caroline. Reminds me how lonesome I am without her.

I was sketching the lone elm when I heard a voice: "Shade only one side of the tree trunk. It will truly come to life."

I turned to find a skinny-looking man, a Mr. St. Clair. At first I was most put off, then soon came to find out he's an artist! A real artist! Caroline would not believe me for a second, but I've seen his drawings, and they are magnificent. Such feeling, with just a few simple lines. And he does it all left-handed. And fast!

This Mr. St. Clair journeys with the traders to make sketches of trail life. He especially hopes to see

Indians. I'm sure he's the only one, besides Jem. He claims he should like to sketch a buffalo hunt!!

Later again

Mama doesn't speak much, except to complain about the mosquitoes. I can tell by the set of her jaw she's not pleased with the trip. I overheard her telling Mr. Ryder this is no place for children.

Speaking of children, have I failed to mention, Diary, that Mama is with child? I see her pressing her belly in places which puts me in mind of testing a watermelon for ripeness. It'll be months till the wee babe is ripe!

I have begun a quilt for the baby, one with twelve patches and each block tells some part of our journey. I asked Mama, "How do you sew a mosquito?" and showed her what I had done. She said, "Can't you give it a long nose or something? You made that little devil look awfully pretty!" and we laughed.

I can see the laugh disappear and Mama's face pinch as the wagon hits ruts and bumps up and down or sways sideways back and forth. It's all she can do not to be ill.

I pray the baby is a girl. Jem prays for a brother.

(Jem often forgets to pray, so I hope more girl prayers ascend to Heaven!)

June 6

Prairie life begins, at last! I should have thought the prairie dead quiet, but there's noise all about. Not just Jem's constant pratter, but the cracking of whips, lowing of cattle, braying of mules, whooping and hollering of the men. It amuses me to see grown men behave like they're forever at a party, but Mama thinks it "disagreeable" to hear so much swearing!

I got Joe-cakes sizzling in the pan for breakfast by the time Mama woke. I think maybe she was a little proud of me. We call them Joe-cakes after Papa. His name was Joseph and Mama says he made the best cornmeal pancakes in the world. When I was little, Mama told me he would make them into shapes for me, like a mountain one time, or a butterfly.

Mr. Ryder insisted they're called johnnycakes. I explained the whole story, insisting back they're called Joe-cakes in this family. He complained that neither did they take so much salt, and we should be sparing to make it last, so I sprinkled extra onto his when he wasn't looking.

Mama saw. She smiled, in the old way.

Noon

One of the mules broke away, chains, harness, and all, with three men chasing him. Not a one could stop him for half an hour! What a race. One of the men finally did catch the bridle, but the stubborn animal would not be led. So he walked backwards all the way to camp, with his capturer on the end of a tether. Jem had himself a good laugh, especially when Mr. Ryder said I'm as stubborn as that mule, and that I would have done the very same!

I like to think of it as strong-willed.

June 6, Camp No. 1, Lone Elm (35 miles from Independence)

When night falls, we set up camp. Tonight is our first real camp, one of many along the trail! With each camp, I'll have a chance to write as supper's cooking.

We formed two circles with our wagons. Inside the

circles, the mules were let to graze, and we started the cooking fires. Before dark, some boys Jem met played leapfrog and a ball game called dare base in the no-man's-land between the two circles. I was the only girl, and those boys thought I couldn't play any ball games. But I can hit as far as any trader's son, and run fast as greased lightning, especially with my skirts newly hemmed to make them a daring two inches shorter!

It almost felt like home. Except for no Caroline.

Suppertime

After the game, the boys were running around hooting and hollering when I spotted a patch of night poppies. Far as I can tell, these pretty little white flowers bloom at night, when the shadows start to fall. I looked up and saw two girls from the second circle of wagons gathering flowers, too, but just as I was about to say hello, someone called, "Eliza, Louisa!" and they went running.

Two girls! Perhaps my own age! I'll sure be on the lookout for them tomorrow.

Fried ham and eggs was our first dinner on the prairie. Breakfast at night, under the stars!

Bedtime

Mama and Mr. Ryder have pitched a tent. Jem and I have our own, a real tent like ones they use in the army, Jem says. It has a pole in the center with a table attached. Mama remarked, "It's a clever table that has only one leg!" She acts more satisfied with things when we stop being in motion.

Jem and I crawled inside. The tent was safe-feeling, spreading its dark wings over us. My bed is nothing but a blanket on the ground, and I can feel every rock and root making itself known.

Mostly it's quiet except for coyotes and Frenchie's snoring under the wagon next to ours. His snores are louder than his swearing!

I fall to sleep every night hearing Jem repeat the same prayer: "Please God, may I look upon your face one day. Amen."

I wrap myself in a buffalo hide, not because I'm cold but for the weight of it. One breath of the sleep-scented hide and I think I hear thunderous hooves, like those Mr. Ryder has told us about. I close my eyes and I am Buffalo Girl, amidst a magnificent herd in the heart of the prairie.

June 7, morning

Up by 7:00. So much bouncing in the wagon, I think all the bones in my body have been shuffled like a deck of cards and rearranged new.

Noon

Nooned at Big Bull Creek, where we ate crackers. That, Mama says, is supposed to be our whole meal! No sight of any Louisa or Eliza. Maybe it was one of those mirages they speak of out here on the prairie. Well, I'm not giving up hope. I know what I saw!

Night, Camp No. 2

I have seen my first shooting star!

June 8, 49 miles from Independence

Mama usually rides in the spring seat, knitting as the wagon bumps along. I tried keeping her company, but it's near impossible to make neat stitches with the rocking of the wagon. Mama doesn't usually stray far from her perch, but today we came to some rocky bluffs overlooking a river. She stood at the top to get a view of things, and surprised me by calling out, "Hellooo!" It came back, *Hel-lo, hel-lo, hel-lo,* ringing around us like a church choir.

Mama said those rocks were called Maiden's Leap. Then she told me a most strange and haunting story:

"Once, an Indian girl wanted to marry a hunter. But her parents wanted her to marry another man, a warrior who had been brave at battle. On the day they were to be wed, the Indian girl came and stood on these very bluffs and raised her hands to the sky and sang a sad song to her beloved hunter. Then she threw herself off the cliff, into the river! But her song, it came echoing back off the cliffs to her loved one. He thought she was calling to him, and ran to meet her. Alas, he was too late."

I leaned far over the bank trying to see into the water, clear to the bottom. Trying to imagine what it would be like to be that Indian girl. Until Mama pulled me back to this world.

Evening, before supper. Camp No. 3.
Black Jack

We struck camp at Black Jack. Fourteen miles from the last camp. Getting toward evening, Mama sits in the wagon and peels potatoes like she was home in our own yellow kitchen. Being tired of cooking, I took a ramble and picked countless wildflowers, then picked some more of Mama's favorite until I practically had me a flower museum!

"Where'd you find cornflowers?" I heard a voice say. I looked up and sure enough, there were two real-life girls by the names of Louisa and Eliza Nutting. Louisa is nearly fourteen and Eliza ten, with me right in the middle. Louisa knows the names of all the flowers, and when she says them, it sounds like a song.

Larkspur and bellflower, lupine and rose. And my favorite: the wild purple aster with its tiny sun face. Louisa said if we don't know the name of a flower, we'll just make one up. Here are some names we thought of:

Sweet cup
Hourglass
Flaming star

Bear's lip
Sneeze weed
Pink-haired pinecone

The last and funniest, named by Eliza, does indeed look like a tiny pine cone with fuzzy pink hair!

Louisa aims to name all her own children after flowers. Violet, Rose, Cordelia (is that a flower, it sounds like one!), and Eliza said, "If you have a boy child, you can name him Sneeze Weed!" I laughed so hard, I think I did sneeze!

Eliza is redheaded, and likes to collect pink pebbles, which she finds most curious. When I asked what should we do with all these flowers, Eliza said, "Crush them in a book." I think she means to press them for safekeeping, which is just what I've done between these pages.

Oh, how I hope to have a red-haired sister one day. I'll teach her all the prairie flowers, and show her how I pressed some in my journal before she was born. Mr. Ryder has made known his wishes that a girl-baby be called Edwina (Ed-wee-na!), after his own mother. It's my duty as big sister to save her from that cruel fate!

Bedtime

The Nuttings are to camp right next to us, in our own wagon circle! Oh, to have a friend again. Better yet, two friends!

June 9, morning

A trader arrived this morning from Bent's Fort, which I heard him say is up the big Arkansas River. He has traded with the Indians and hauls wagon loads of skins on his way back to Missouri. He told Mr. Ryder and Mr. Nutting about the road and river crossings, and said the Indians'll be thick once we get to Pawnee Fork.

Later I got Jem to ask Mr. Ryder how far to Pawnee Fork. Mr. Ryder has his faults, but he sure does know this trail.

He said 298 miles. 298 miles! We are already a million miles from anywhere!

Just on evening

Six o'clock and we are still not on our way. One of the rear wagons is caught in a mud hole, and it takes several teams (and what feels like forever) to pull it out. Time stretches like thread spilling from a spool on this prairie — one day can feel like a month.

Camp No. 4

Not sure where we are. Prairie, is all. Mr. Ryder says a good camp has water, wood, and grass. There is plenty of the latter!

Late night

Tonight I was started awake by a most eerie sound. It sounded like cat-dog-sheep-wolf all together. Jem called it wolves, but I had already conjured up images of a four-headed beast with sixteen legs and the jaws of a dragon. Mr. Biscuit flew out with a bark and drove them away. Mr. B, good dog, sleeps now between Jem and me, but I'm afraid those wolves have chased off sleep for me.

June 10

Up at 4 A.M. when we heard the call, "Roll out!" Mama is having her morning time again. Up to me to blow on the coals and start the fire and see to breakfast. I first roast the coffee beans over the fire, then set water to boil. Does Mr. Ryder even notice that she eats nothing but crackers? If I am stubborn, he is blind.

After breakfast we had just started out when we seized upon the skeleton of a papoose. It had been buried on a platform in a tree, and fallen. It was shrunken and withered as a dried-up plum, wrapped all in a red handkerchief, blue flannels, and a buffalo robe. I could not pull my eyes away from those bones, pale as the prairie moon.

Mama called, "Get in the wagon and ride a bit, Florrie. Before you know it, your feet'll be spreading out wider than Joe-cakes from all that walking."

We're sitting quiet now. I can't shake the image of that tiny skeleton. Keep thinking I hear a lullaby in between the blowing dust. Ever since laying eyes on the papoose, Mama rubs her newly swollen belly with a different gaze on her face, which says she's about to behold a miracle. Mr. Ryder doesn't see it, nor does Jem, but you can't miss it if you're a pupil of things, as I am.

I wonder, did she have the miracle look for me, too?

Noon on the prairie

Too hot to write. Now I do feel like a mule, hanging my tongue out, panting with thirst.

Night

Too hot to sleep.

June 11

Our first Sabbath on the prairie!

Quiet as a church without singing. Jem says he's not heard one swear all the day. Every now and again I hear *wee wee wee wee wee*, the sharp whistle of the partridge, the *guggle guggle* of the warbler, or the sweet chirp of the lark. Mr. Ryder knows them all and calls to them like a fellow feathered friend. Today a lark answered back. *Twee! Twee!* Fancy that! Our own Mr. Ryder, a lark.

I do like Mr. Ryder on the Sabbath. (I will have to add bird calling to my list of his good points.) He is altogether more relaxed and attentive to Mama. Jem tried to imitate the birdsong, too, a raven's caw, but it sounded more like a sick cow.

June 12, 110-mile Creek

Left trees behind. Scarcely a bush or shrub to break the horizon. The grass is so tall in places as to hide Mr. Ryder's waist and nearly all but Jem's head. Mama says this prairie reminds her of the sea, the way it goes on for miles and miles and miles. To think I did not know my own mama has been to the sea! I told Mama if all this grass were sea, I would swim and swim and swim. I would swim all the way to New Mexico.

June 13

Picked berries with Louisa and Eliza. We found any number of raspberries and gooseberries on the banks of the creek. We even fixed a line and tried fishing with Jem. Nothing bites but the mosquitoes. I do believe all the fish in Kansas must have gone to California.

Louisa seemed content NOT to catch a single fish. Eliza showed us her purple tongue and said, "My belly's too full of berries to fit any fish!"

Later

Our small fire let off sparks like shooting stars. I was sorry Mama could not stay up to be with us. Louisa played her violin for us! She played it smooth as silk — not one squeak! As soon as it grew dark, we sang songs like "Yankee Doodle" and Mr. Ryder's favorite, "The Blue Bells of Scotland."

Mr. Nutting showed Eliza and me a funny dance, and even Jem did the jig, though he looked more like he was stepping on hot coals from the fire. Quite a merry mood was in the smoky air.

Jem pleaded with Mr. Ryder to tell us a story. Eliza and Louisa had never heard any of his tales before, and they gazed upon him spellbound, like a real actor in a theater play.

What a tall tale! About a giant who eats bread made of iron and crushes stone like it was cheese.

Jem begged me to tell it again before bed, but he fell asleep just as I was getting to the good part. If he dreams of ugly, stone-crushing giants, it's not my fault!

Middle of the night

A most frightful thing! My hands are still shaking, and my heart beating wildly.

I couldn't fall asleep, so I slipped out of the tent and climbed into the wagon. With only the full moon to light my way, I still knew precisely where to find Papa's trunk. I gingerly lifted the lid, trying all the while not to make a sound.

I lifted out his red flannel overshirt, which smelled of soap and pine. I wrapped the arms around me. I found Papa's worn-down boots, a handkerchief, and a belt knife. His soft, wide-brimmed felt hat came down over my eyes when I tried it on.

I cast about looking for the cornmeal barrel, thinking how sweet just a finger lick of honey would taste right then.

Next thing I knew, I was blinded by a light, a shotgun pointed right between my eyes!

How my heart raced when I saw my twelve short years pass before me, without so much as a good-bye to Mama and Jem.

Then the words, "You there! Thief!" finally hit me, in a voice I recognized. The man pointing the gun at me was none other than Mr. Ryder himself!

June 14, first light

The rest of last night is a blur. Mr. Ryder yelling at me something awful. Mama in her nightshirt yelling back at him. Jem standing outside the tent squeezing his eyes shut and covering his ears.

After the yelling, I hugged myself under the buffalo robe, feeling my own life come back into my blood. A stare-down contest with a gun sure does make a person feel lucky to be alive.

Mr. Ryder's horse kicked him first thing this morning. Made him a bit lame. That's the honest truth! Mama whispered to me, "That horse must be smarter than we thought!" She's not keen on Mr. Ryder pointing guns at everything and anyone. I rewarded Velvet with an apple.

Midday

Later, Jem and I were walking in front of the wagons when a beautiful little animal caught our attention in the distance. I thought it was a dog at first. Jem said it was nothing more than a boulder in the road. Mr. Ryder lent us his spyglass, partly to settle the argument and partly to make nice for nearly shooting me last night.

What was it? A curious antelope! More timid of us two-leggers than we were of it. Its dark, clear eyes pleaded like to make friends.

Can an antelope be lonely?

Later. Camp No. 9. Bluff Creek Camp

This evening, I was sewing a lark on my quilt. All the while, Eliza was watching me as intent as a heron on a fish, like she'd never seen a needle and thread before.

I thought maybe she was trying to learn sewing when she piped up, "I know where we can see a real canary that sings." Turns out there's a trader's wife who keeps to her wagon by the name of Mrs. Ernestine Wilcox. They say that she would not leave her St. Louis home without her thirteen canary birds! Oh, how I long to lay eyes on them and hear their song. Eliza said, "Let's go tomorrow and spy on them." Then Louisa said, "You two act like foolish children," after which she admitted she wants to come, too.

Eliza also reported that Mrs. Wilcox has with her a cook who tells fortunes. How that girl knows is beyond me. What a spy she'd make for soldiers in the army!

I don't know which is more exciting: thirteen songbirds from St. Louis, or the prospect of knowing my own future.

June 15, Noon rest

Sakes alive! What an adventure. Eliza came and reported that Mrs. Wilcox leaves her wagon and goes down to the creek to get water when we stop for our midday rest. Louisa and I agreed it was the perfect time to sneak up and spy on the canaries. We carefully stepped round the back of dozens of other wagons, until we came to one that had ST. LOUIS written on the outside cover.

"What if someone thinks we're stealing?" asked Louisa, but we made her shush before she could get our nerves up.

We waited silently to make sure no one was about. As soon as we determined it safe, Eliza pulled back the wagon cover and we all three peered inside. There, in a cage atop a bureau, were the sun-yellow songbirds, merrily chirping as if singing for us were their purpose in this life.

Eliza sang a high-pitched note or two back, and Louisa and I joined her. Such a sweet symphony we caused that I jumped and Louisa screamed when a voice behind us said, "Birds without a cage cannot fly fast enough!"

Louisa and I did find wings on our feet. How we ran! But Eliza, she did not follow us. We hid behind a tree and waited. When Eliza finally came to us, I asked, "That person who speaks in riddles, who *was* that?" To which Eliza did answer, "The fortune-teller!"

As I sit here now, I still can't believe Eliza has spoken with the fortune-teller! My heart near thumped out of my chest just thinking about it. The woman turned on her angry-like and asked, "Why does this bird not fly?" and Eliza piped right up and said, "I would like to know my future, ma'am," after which the woman said, "The future is a long ways away and looks different in the daylight. Gotta be dark to see that far."

Eliza says she stood there frowning a frown until the woman said, "When you think you're ready, bring one object special to you and meet me at the campfire after dark."

"May I bring my sister and my friend, too?" Eliza asked.

"Yes, indeed-y," said the woman. "Tell 'em come with their eyes closed and hearts open."

Eliza Nutting must be the bravest girl I have ever known!

Soon we'll know our futures — perhaps tomorrow night.

June 16

Hot today

Caliente.

Hot, hotter, hottest. (Reminds me of my lessons back home at the School of the Sacred Heart.)

Later

Hotter still. Pulled off all but my chemise! I don't care beans who sees me like so. It's hot as a sizzling Joe-cake on the fry pan, and though Mama says I'm prone to exaggeration, I don't believe this is one.

Even Mama seems to be sinking further and further into the folds of her bonnet. She burns easy. My arms are so brown, I hardly recognize them as my own.

Too hot to pick berries. Too hot to fish.

Evening

The heat is shimmery, like grease in a pan, and forms small clouds around people and things and trees.

I think I saw a mirage today, right in the middle of the trail! First it was a party of Indians on horseback. Next I was certain there were no Indians at all, but a tall castle, with a tower and flags flying. Then I squinted and saw a blue lake with white sands and lapping water. I thought to take a swim, but when I unsquinted my eyes, the lake was gone.

The heat visits some strange happenings upon us.

Night

Tonight we made ready to meet the fortune-teller. I asked God to forgive me for lying to Mama and telling her instead that I was taking biscuits to Mrs. Wilcox, who had taken ill. Mama would not approve of fortune-telling, but I think God, if He is all knowing, can understand better than anybody the need for seeing into the unknown.

Louisa took a lock of hair. I took Papa's hat. I've

taken to wearing it now, favoring it over my bonnet. Mr. Ryder says it's most unladylike, for which I love it all the more. Eliza would not tell what she had hidden in her apron pocket.

As soon as we came to the campfire, the fortune-teller led Eliza into her tent. When she emerged, we nearly pounced on her to find out what happened, but she said only that she was not allowed to tell until we had seen the fortune-teller ourselves.

My turn came next. My heart thump-thumped again as I hunched over and stepped into the tent. The fortune-teller asked me to scat myself cross-legged on the ground directly across from her. When she asked for my special object, I took off Papa's hat and handed it to her. Then I closed my eyes and tried to open my heart like she asked. I swear I felt a most unusual breeze come across my face and through my hair. I couldn't help but wonder all the time if Papa was going to speak to me or some such.

Instead, the fortune-teller spoke to me in a deep voice. She explained she was about to reveal to me a secret between me and myself that I must hold in my heart. I prepared for my secret with a hopeful heart, only to be reminded that the fortune-teller sure speaks some nonsense!

The moment we were out of earshot, we laughed like fools and busted out with the telling of our secrets.

Louisa was told: *A blade of grass pushes against an obstacle as it sprouts from the earth.*

Eliza's secret: *Horse and wagon part — all things separate and unite.*

My own fortune: *She who sees clouds and thunder knows that rain fills the air.*

I fail to see what the weather has to do with my future?!

June 17

RAIN!

The fortune-teller was right! About the weather, anyway. Finally the heat is broken.

Traveled all day in rain. At last the dust is washed from me. My tongue's been parchment for a week. Jem and I caught raindrops on our tongues. The rain tasted better than a tall, cool glass of raspberry vinegar lemonade, the way Mama used to make it.

*　　*　　*

I have seen my first Indians! Three men and two women. They were quite friendly. The men and women dress almost alike. Some had their faces painted. We gave them food, and they turned to go quite peaceful and all. I wonder where all the talk of scalping and poison arrows and war whooping comes from?

A short distance later I saw one of their houses. It was made of branches, with a hole at the top for smoke to go out so they can cook inside over a fire. Very clever!

I wonder what they think of us. I only hope the men will not be hunting too many of the Indians' buffalo. I admit to wrapping myself in a warm robe at night, but I do not care to eat such great creatures.

Camp No. 12, Council Grove

This place is thick with trees, so we have stopped here for a few days to gather timber. Frenchie and the others cut wood and lash it beneath the wagon for the journey. Also we need time to repair the wagons and rest the animals.

I for one am glad for the rest.

Just when I thought I could sketch or go find Louisa and Eliza, Mama has me elbow-deep in washing clothes. There's so much lathering of soap and slopping of water, I told Mama, "I feel like I'm washing clothes for an army!" Mama said, "Mr. Ryder and Jem do seem to make up their own army, don't they?" It was nice, how we laughed. Just us.

I think I caught Mama missing Papa's quiet, but all she did was scrub harder.

The men prepare their firearms. I hope all this fuss is for shooting small game and not Indians.

Jem says they should call this place Council Grave, with so many Indians about. How his head's filled up with stories! Mr. Ryder says this place gets its name from a big meeting held here between traders and Indians to help keep peace and safety. I pray that all the Indians in these parts did indeed go to this so-called peace meeting.

Afternoon

Mr. Biscuit and I have come upon Mr. St. Clair, who has made a most handsome sketch of Indians at a ceremonial dance. How I wish I could capture such likeness. And to think he makes dozens of such sketches before painting one picture. The artist re-marked, "Anyone can draw, with a little practice and determination." To which I replied, "I think I'll stay a student of nature. People are much too difficult to draw."

"Start with Mr. Biscuit," the artist told me. "If you can get him to sit still long enough to sketch his portrait, that is." He laughed till his ears wiggled. Then he surprised me by ripping the sketch right from his book and handing it over to me. I protested, of course, but he insisted I keep it for study!

A real artist's drawing!

June 18, still at Council Grove

Today I could not help but leave Mama to the washing so I could go off exploring with Louisa and Eliza. We scrambled up a steep bank to get a good view, and saw a scene more beautiful than any art-ist could draw. Wildflowers such as the red painted-cup, yellow goldenpea and rose-purple fairyslipper made a patchwork threaded with silvery green grasses. We felt like we'd been painted into a landscape ourselves.

From on top the hill we could see the heads of our city of wagons. Eliza said our caravan looked no bigger than a spider.

We found a pool filled with the most crystal-clear, cold liquid any of the three of us has ever known. Louisa found the words BIG JOHN'S SPRING carved in a nearby tree, looking as if they were cut with a tomahawk. I thought Big John must be a friend of Mr. Ryder's giant. Eliza thought him a blackhearted pirate, and Louisa suspected him to be a famous horse thief.

Everything around us looked wild and twiny, until I thought Big John himself might be lurking, waiting to lunge at us through the grapevines.

We drank our fill. No water on this earth could be more satisfying.

We then heard a rustling in the thicket and flew down that hill. I don't think we could have gone faster with a pack of wild wolves at our heels.

When I got back to camp, Mama was most distressed, and not only over the wash still to be done. She scolded me something awful and says I have to learn different now that we're entering Indian territory. She made me stay in the tent, where I'm bound to think over my misdeeds. I am not to see Louisa and Eliza or join the campfires tonight.

I am sore angry for the scolding, but grateful, too. No more washing for the rest of this day!

later

What a life! To be shut up in a tent by my own self with the rain pouring down fierce as a wolf pack on the run.

Must tell Mr. St. Clair about the view from the hill, but I'm trapped here.

Water runs through the tent like a stream, making mud of the ground. As if a pack of pigs has been wallowing inside the tent.

All I could think to amuse myself then was to take up sewing my quilt. I'm working on a patch of the view from the bluffs at Big John's Spring for the baby, even though Mama would hardly approve.

But when I went to take it up, it was missing. *¡Perdido!* Gone!

I bet I know the thief. Jem. He's hidden it just to vex me, so I have nothing to do but sew, kept here like a prisoner.

Now it has commenced to lightning! As if God is sore angry with me, not just Mama.

June 19. Diamond Spring (12 miles from CG)

Up at six and a half o'clock. Still being punished by Mama, who is chillier to me than water from Diamond Spring.

While I was boiling coffee this morning, I caught Eliza reading my diary!

I marched directly over to the Nuttings' wagon and gave that girl a piece of my mind. What was she thinking — looking at my own private thoughts without asking?

She protested (of course), claiming that she did not read a word. Only opened my book to the back to have a look at the fairyslipper we found yesterday. She knew I would have pressed it there.

I will not repeat the angry words I returned.

She said I was a hateful person for thinking so little of her. And she is resolved never to speak to me again.

That makes two of us! Ouch! What a day this is!

Later

More rain. And rain and rain. Stuck. Again. We came to a crossing where a small creek swelled like a full belly. Our wagon was sorely bogged down. I jumped out and waded in the creek, thinking I was helping to lighten the load, but Mama only snapped at me for risking my neck. I fail to see what my neck has to do with it, when the water came only as high as my waist. I offered then to throw off a chair, or chest, or churn, to which I got nothing but a stony glare from her.

Nothing I do is right.

June 20

On our way to Lost Spring. An apt name. I feel lost. Like a stick figure drawn in the dust, erased by wagon tracks.

Later

I have uncovered the thief! Not Jem in the least. The thief's name is none other than — Mr. Biscuit! That silly hound carried off my quilt and hid it under Mama's good kitchen table for his own bed.

How on earth will I free my handiwork of doggy hair and slobber?

Mama and I were bent over the cooking fire (still not talking) when Jem called out to us. We turned our eyes to heaven and saw a magnificent rainbow. The sky was on fire with colors.

"If there is a pot of gold at the end of the rainbow," Jem said, "I bet it must be all the way in California. And I aim to find it someday."

Mama laughed. Her laugh, though not for me, was as welcome as a change of clothes.

The trail, like a rainbow, leads us west.

And west. And westward still.

Later still

Mr. St. Clair has made several new drawings. He calls them his field sketches. I asked him how he came to be such an artist. He said, "I was an orphan at the age of fourteen. After my parents died, I had to make a living for myself, so I became a sign painter. That was the beginning."

I have also seen him paint pictures in color and draw detailed maps. He's been all the way to California, Oregon, and back, sketching all the while. He's risked his life many times just to paint Indians! Once he even traveled with mountain man Kit Carson himself, making maps along the way.

I must remember to tell Jem!

Camp No. 14, Lost Spring, nighttime

Still angry with Eliza. Then Louisa came and pleaded her case. She convinced me Eliza meant no harm. I missed my friend, so I went to make amends, but could not find her.

Louisa said, "That girl has a mind of her own and a heart for exploration. She could be off to anywhere."

June 21

Mud, mud, and more mud.

One mile per hour is all the time we made today.
No wood. No water.
Hungry. Tired of wet clothes.

Passed a wagon stuck fast in a mud hole with the tongue twisted off, belonging to a trader, name of

Cutter. He had two other wagons stuck, and his team gave out from having no water.

I was sure we'd stop to help, but Mr. Ryder insisted we push on to make camp before nightfall. I don't think Mr. Nutting agreed with him. Seems to me mighty hard out here to tell when to think of others, and when to take care of one's own skin.

Camp No. 15, Cottonwood Creek

Made camp but are now stuck here in mud. Waiting out rain. Mr. Ryder told us a story to pass the time. The story turned out to be not about giants, but a true-life murder!

It goes that there was a well-known trader by the name of Elliott. He was a rich man, known for his store full of goods and the way he always traded fair with folks. One night two men came into his store pretending they aimed to trade, but when Mr. Elliott turned his back to reach for a hide, the bad men stabbed him in the back and killed him and made off with most of his goods and all his money. The only thing they didn't see fit to stealing was his Bible, which was all his family had left of him.

Now the reason Mr. Ryder brings this up is that we passed a wagon train headed for Missouri that carries a trader up from Chihuahua, right where it happened. And this trader is supposedly wearing a gold watch that bears an exact likeness to that which belonged to Mr. Elliott!

To think! There could be a murderer in our midst, camping in the same spot as us tonight.

June 22, a wretched day

Eliza is missing! Mrs. Nutting is beside herself with worry. Eliza went off to the creek before breakfast and has not returned. No one has seen her for hours. Louisa assured her mama it's just like Eliza to wander off and not tell a soul. I hope she's right. My heart quickens at the thought of the murderer, and it's all I can do to push the image from my mind.

Evening

Supper is over. Still no Eliza.

Later

Getting dark and Eliza did not make it back to the campfire. It's not like her to miss stories and dancing. Of course, there will be no dancing tonight.

With darkness falling, Mr. Nutting has organized a search party. Mr. Ryder has gone, and has taken Jem and Mr. Biscuit with him and the others. I feel helpless . . . I'm no good at waiting.

Later still

Well past dark.

Waiting. Waiting. They've been gone several hours now. What if something has happened to her? What if she's not found? What if the rain doesn't let up?

What if? What if? What if?

Going on midnight

The men are back. Wet and weary. Eliza is nowhere. Rain doesn't help. They can't even see tracks with so much mud. We wait for daylight, and the rain to let up.

So tired, I can't sleep. I'm sure if I close my eyes the

rain will give me a drowning in my sleep. Or worse yet, a murderer!

June 23, morning

Rain stopped at last. The men went up the creek at first light, in search of Eliza. Even Jem slipped out before breakfast without my notice. I should've been awake, keeping thoughts of Eliza awake with me.

Louisa and I wonder, "Is this what the fortune-teller meant, 'Horse is separated from the wagon'?" We're off to find the woman and see if she knows what's happened to Eliza.

Late morning

Been to see the fortune-teller without objects or anything. She told us, "Don't you worry . . . horse and wagon belong together. Save room in your hearts for thoughts of her now. She'll be needing that more than your worried heads."

Louisa got a scolding for leaving the wagon. Mrs. Nutting does not want Louisa to leave her sight. I brought my sewing over to sit with them. Six patches so far, including the rainbow I'm working on. Sure is hard to get a mind onto neat stitches when all I can do is think of Eliza.

Noon

The men have come back from their searching for some coffee and something to fill their bellies. They say no news could be good news, but it's hard to believe them, looking all downcast. Blown-down branches from the storm litter every path, and there's mud everywhere and they can't seem to pick up a single sign of her.

Night

Another night passes without Eliza.

June 24, morning

Eliza has been missing a full two days now. It's getting harder to keep up hope.

Captain Elias is most anxious to be back on the trail now that the weather's cleared a bit. I fear that if Eliza is not found soon, our captain will make us push on without the Nuttings. I could not bear it. To think that I accused her falsely of wrongdoing, and left her feeling so hateful toward me. Now I may never see that dear sweet girl again. I feel helpless as a baby bird blown from the nest. Mama says all we can do is pray to God she'll be returned safely to us.

Jem returned with news: They found an apron full of pinecones that looked to be Eliza's! Mrs. Nutting wept when she saw it, confirming that it is for sure and certain Eliza's own apron. Nobody could speak. I'm afraid we were all thinking the worst.

I heard Mama tell Mrs. Nutting she was sure it had to be a good sign.

In the midst of our worry over Eliza, Jem went and nearly got himself bit by a rattler. In his haste to report to us on Eliza's apron, he stepped on a snake with eleven rattles! He stood still as stone with eyes so wide, they near swallowed up his face. Mama did not hesitate to kill the snake with a stick.

Jem walked backwards and took hold of my hand. We, the rest of us, kept a safe distance, staring at the dead snake.

Suddenly, that dead snake opened its mouth wide, and out jumped a fat brown toad. For a moment, it stood blinking its eyes at us, then went hopping off into the grass like nothing.

How we all did laugh right over top of our worry. Eliza would have laughed the loudest.

June 24, afternoon, a great day!

Eliza is found!

I could hardly tear myself away from Eliza's side, but I had to write her story down as it was told to me, with Mr. Biscuit as the hero of our tale:

Eliza was wandering around picking berries and collecting pinecones when she got farther and farther away from camp. Soon she didn't recognize where she was, and the harder she tried to get back, the more confused she got. She tried calling out but was afraid Indians might hear her instead of us.

The rain was coming down hard, so she crawled into a space between two rocks and put branches over her head to keep dry and hidden. She tucked in like a duck asleep that whole night through.

The next morning she ate all the berries she could find, but was still so hungry, she nearly ate a pinecone!

Then coming on evening as she was still trying to find her way back, she spied some animal tracks in the mud and bent to study them. Sooner than you can say "jack rabbit," she turned to find a strange black-and-white-striped critter upon her, more fierce than a wolf! Eliza started to run, and before she knew it, she had climbed a tree to safety. That critter would not forget her and leave her alone. It pawed and clawed at that tree and hissed with a terrible snarl all the while.

Eliza's heart was thumping away, but what could she do? She spent the whole night up in that tree afraid to come down. By now her hair was all in a snarl (her temper, too!) and her dress torn to ribbons.

It seemed like a week till she heard Mr. Biscuit barking and barking, right at the foot of her tree. Eliza called out to Mr. B, daring to hope at last she'd been saved. Mr. Biscuit raced back and led the others to the spot, all the while barking up a storm, then sniffed out that wild animal until Mr. Nutting came and shot it dead.

Mr. Ryder exclaimed, "I do believe we caught ourselves a badger."

The mud-streaked Eliza said, "Don't be fooled for a minute by the size of that critter. I'd rather come face-to-face with a buffalo any day!"

This concludes Act I of the drama of Eliza Nutting and her run-in with a wild badger. I told Eliza we could make a play about it and take parts, but she said, "Only if I don't have to play the part of myself!"

June 25, noontime

Eliza and I are all made up now. I'll pray to God each night for a long time to come, thanking him for returning Eliza to us in one piece.

Mrs. Nutting paid Mr. St. Clair to make her a portrait of Louisa and Eliza. They sit for him at the noon rest while he draws. I wonder if this is Mrs. Nutting's way of keeping her Eliza close.

Eliza has trouble sitting still. Even so, she makes a much better pupil than Mr. Biscuit! I'm still trying to get him right, but he always comes out looking pointy as a fox.

Mr. St. Clair has given me a special thick pencil for shading. When I asked him how soon he would be needing it back, he replied, "Keep it till you've learned something."

Afternoon

Jem climbed a cliff with Mr. Biscuit and stumbled on a grove of plum trees. I'm afraid he didn't leave many plums behind. He's eaten handfuls, and they were not ripe — now he curls up on the ground like a dry leaf. Moaning and groaning and clutching his stomach. Mama brewed him some pennyroyal tea, with hot ginger.

Even Mr. Biscuit ate a plum! That dog is getting heaps of attention, now that he helped Eliza get saved. He sure is looking fat and sleepy, with all the niblets folks are giving him for his good works.

I should have liked to taste plums, but not if it makes me squeal like a baby pig!

Camp No. 16. Cottonwood. coming on evening

The cottonwood trees along the river are tall and majestic, tall enough to rival Mr. Ryder's giants. They lean toward one another like gossiping old women. Great dark turkeys fly overhead and perch in their branches.

There's one old tree stump with a funny shape — splintered, looks the way I imagine a cactus to be.

Frenchie, the head driver, told Jem and me that each cottonwood has its own spirit. A bit like a ghost.

Frenchie says there goes an old story in which a certain cottonwood was thought to protect travelers along this trail. Then one night a terrible rainstorm came and lightning hit the tree and it fell into the current. Before the current carried it away, the spirit of the tree could be heard crying! One part of it clung to the earth while the other part was carried away by the current.

That tree reminds me of me. One part of me clings to Missouri. To my old life with Caroline and the School of the Sacred Heart and the house with real floorboards that held my father's footsteps.

The other part of me rides the wind — like a leaf.

After dark

I kept a cottonwood leaf to press in my journal so I can show Eliza and Louisa. Frenchie gave me a seed pod from the cottonwood — a pear-shaped capsule half an inch long. He says the capsule holds about thirty seeds. It's in my pocket till I find a safe place for it. I'll keep it and plant my own cottonwood grove when I get to New Mexico. If I give some to Louisa and Eliza, maybe they'll plant cottonwoods when they reach California. Then one day we'll be old ladies rocking in our chairs looking at sister trees.

I told the story of the cottonwood spirit crying at campfire tonight. Mama said, "It must have been the wind rustling the leaves, don't you think?" She may be right, but in my heart I believe it was the tree spirit.

June 26. Camp No. 17

No water. No wood.

June 27

I'm sad to recount here the oxen are dying of thirst. No water within five miles, and now they can't move except to hunch under the wagons for shade. Frenchie tried applying a cool mud plaster to one, but the poor beast wandered off into deep grass in search of water. Another poor creature fell in the road and the teamster gave him up for dead.

To think only days ago we were bogged down in mud.

Mr. St. Clair sketches them with a madness. I wonder how he finds the heart for sketching such misery.

Evening. Camp No. 18

The oxen we are left with can't seem to pull the slightest load. Mr. Ryder began throwing off our belongings to make it easier on them.

There went our cookstove and several pots and pans, the old rosewood rocker, sacks of flour and barrels of beans. Even the barrel of cornmeal full of Mama's fine dishes. I was scarcely able to rescue Aunt Florence's honey jar and hide it before Mr. Ryder hurled the barrel out onto the trail.

No sooner had I rescued my honey jar than I turned to see Mr. Ryder heave Papa's trunk over his head and toss it out of the wagon!

I flung myself at him, too late. I leaped from the wagon in haste, twisting my leg and falling back on my ankle, crying out in pain. Dragging my leg behind me, I crawled to Papa's trunk, where his things were scattered in the dust.

Mr. Ryder came and lifted me, kicking and screaming, under the shade of a tree. Mama stayed silent on the matter, her face frozen.

I'd have given anything to hear her scream.

June 28

The river's in sight now.

Still fuming. Not speaking to anyone but Louisa and Eliza. I had to tell them about Papa's things. They're both furious on my behalf. Truer friends a person could not ask for.

Louisa asked, "Will this help you feel better, Florrie?" and held up the picture of Papa from the dusty Bible. Also a squished-up version of Papa's hat.

For once, I was without words.

Noon rest

Jem's busy pretending to whittle, and looking over my shoulder again. "Go hunt an antelope," I told him. He lit up with the thought. "Can't catch an antelope with this," he said, showing me his fishing rod. "Then go catch a whale," I told him. I wanted to be alone with my redhot anger.

"A whale!" His eyes grew wide. "Are there . . . ?" I laughed, a laugh they could've heard in Missouri. Whales in the Arkansas River! I shouldn't tease him so. But I'm feeling dustier than a desert cactus, and about as prickly, too.

The guidebook warns of all sorts of pestilence . . . I don't know if they mean sickness or bugs, but the worst *pestilence* so far is Jem!

Evening, Camp No. 19, Little Arkansas River

Mr. Ryder brought me two strings of licorice. I don't know how he's come by sweets on the prairie. At first I thought licorice a pitiful peace offering. But then I thought of Eliza and made up my mind not to let another sun set on my anger.

Forgiveness is hard work.

June 29, Camp No. 20, on the banks of the Arkansas

The mosquitoes are "disagreeable," a word Mama has made popular since we started this journey. I wonder which is louder: the whining of the insects, or my own complaints? Now my poor ankle is not only near-broken, but ringed with swells from their stings. Some are knots the size of a pea!

I wish I had a silver *peso* for every sting. Mr. Ryder says I am beginning to think like a trader!

I've learned to tuck my feet under me now, and

wrap Mama's shawl over my head, until I think I'll die smothered from heat. Despite the shawl (and my own humming), I still hear the buzz, buzz, BUZZing. All night the slaps travel through the camp — feeble attempts to rid our tents of the pests. The vile creatures have even found their way under my chemise!

Jem has warned me about sleeping with my mouth open. I now clench my teeth and press my lips together before falling to sleep. I hope the Good Lord can still hear my prayer over all the buzzing — deliver me from this plague of plagues!

June 30

Jem is doing some whining of his own. He complains of a ringing in his ear, and has not whittled all day. Mr. Elias, our captain, came and blew tobacco smoke in his ear. It looked like Jem was on fire! I could've a split a cabbage, laughing. Mama did not seem keen on the method, but Jem has stopped his grousing.

July 1. Camp No. 22. Little Cow Creek

249 miles out.

July 2 Along the banks of the Arkansas

I took up sewing my quilt this morning. A little worse for wear now that Mr. Biscuit has had his way with it. No sooner had I begun my stitches than Mama quick reminded me it was Sabbath.

I know she thinks I'm wicked as well as forgetful — that I've turned a blind eye to my own salvation — but truth be told, the days blur one into another on the prairie. It's hard to recognize Sabbath without the ringing of church bells.

So instead of sewing I'll write a poem. Thankfully, taking up my pen is not considered work.

> I am a princess of the prairie.
> I am a pilgrim, far from home.
> I am a pioneer!

We're deep into buffalo country now. Along the trail are many tiny pools, like blue beads strung on a dark brown thread.

"Buffalo wallows," Mr. Nutting called them. "Made by buffalo bulls fighting," he told me. It seems they put their heads together and walk round and round, slowly, making a hollow that catches rainwater.

I find this world a strange place indeed. How can something so lovely come from fighting?

Mr. St. Clair has captured the necklace of pools perfectly. He asked me, "How are you coming with that pencil, Florrie?" I think he meant did I learn something yet.

"I learned that the pencil does not make the artist," I told him, to which he seemed to get a good laugh. "Then you've learned all you need to know," he said.

"Does this mean I'm to return your pencil?" I asked in earnest. To which he laughed even harder, but made no effort to recover his pencil.

Afternoon

For miles, oxen dropped and were left to die. Some still had their eyes open. I didn't want to look but could not help myself. It'd be like not looking at wagon ruts in the road or all the stars in the sky, there's so many. Never have I seen so much death.

Worse yet, we came across an abandoned wagon. When the men looked inside, they found a man and woman dead maybe a day or two. Mr. Elias said right off it was cholera. He knew the signs.

The men discovered a note that let us know those two souls were the Reverend Mitchell Hester and his wife. They read the note aloud to our company.

My dear wife passed on to the Good Lord, the cholera having ravaged her, and I fear I'm not able to hold out much longer. My strength is ebbing. I am ready now and hold nothing against the wagon master for leaving us behind to head for California. Though these earthly eyes may never see the Promised Land on earth, I hope soon to be with my wife in the heavenly kingdom, among the angels.

The Reverend Mitchell Hester

Captain Elias ordered us to stay away from the wagon. He called for the men to bury them quick, and a few of the traders stopped to make a proper grave — as proper as it gets on the prairie. They dug a deep hole to keep the bodies safe from wolves. Then they rolled the dead in blankets, lowered them into the hole, and put stones on top. After they cover them with earth, the cattle are made to tromp over the grave so that no animal (or otherwise) digs it up.

Sendavel, one of the Mexican traders, made a cross

and said, *"Que Dios te bendiga."* God bless you. And somebody made a sign like a headstone marking their passing. Some of the traders wanted to play cards to parcel out the belongings in the wagon, which made Captain Elias madder than a hornet. He commanded them to burn the wagon at once, on account of the cholera.

I couldn't help but wonder if the Hesters had any children.

I was good to Jem for the remainder of the day.

July 3. Left Arkansas River. Crossed Walnut Creek

If you can believe it, I have missed all the excitement, not remembering one wink of it as I had to be plucked from the deep like a fish, having been hit on the head with a bottle!

It was some time before I came to. Mr. Ryder was rubbing my face with awful-smelling whiskey, and Mama, bending over me, appeared to have four eyes. Mama said my first words were, "Where's my hat?"

It all started earlier today when Jem sighted a huge rock in the distance, jutting up from the unbroken prairie like a blot of ink against the sky. Mr. Ryder said it must be fifteen miles or more away. We were most anxious to make the distance.

We got to Ash Creek ahead of the other wagons. Mr. Ryder took a look and said, "Looks innocent enough to me." The water in the creek did not seem high. Mama remarked, "The bank looks awfully steep," but Mr. Ryder meant to cross. We no sooner had started down the bank when Mr. Ryder yelled, "Whoa there! Whoa!" and Frenchie and two others ahead of us tried to stop. We had now reached the edge of the cliff, and Mr. Ryder, thinking it quite safe, called, "Go on!" No sooner had the words left his lips than we were whirled through the air and landed with a CRASH!

The wagon looks somewhat broken to pieces! Jem's arm was caught 'neath a shard of wood and Frenchie rushed to lift him out. When he set Jem back on safe ground, he could see Jem's bone sticking clean out of his arm, and did some terrible twisting, yanking, and doctoring in general to get it back in its rightful place. Jem, they said, bit his bottom lip to bleeding and let out a string of cuss words, for which he didn't even get himself in trouble.

July 4

On the trail for weeks now. Left behind the lush green prairie for buffalo grass.

It's only been a day since Jem spied the rock, but I thought we'd never reach it. At last, on noon, we came to the high mound called Pawnee Rock. One of the other traders said it got its name from a battle fought here between some soldiers and the Pawnee Indians.

Jem and I scrambled up to the top, me reaching it first on account of Jem's bad arm. Buffalo. The prairie's black with them, so many you can hardly see grass.

Jem and I carved our names in the rock. Jem's looks like this:

JEM RYDER

only harder to read since he had to use his left hand.

Mine looks like this:

FLORRIE (MACK) RYDER

Both are a bit shaky. We had to hurry up for fear of Indians.

Mama says we made history today. I must admit to a shiver down my spine, seeing my name and Jem's amidst the many hundreds of others who passed this way, hoping for a different life. Could not help but think of that headstone for the Hesters, and how lucky we are to be marking the living instead of the dead.

Late at night. Camp No. 25

There were no celebrations here, no fireworks to mark the Fourth. It seemed strange passing without fanfare, till tonight — after the fires died down to a soft glow of embers.

Lo and behold, I saw a comet. Its flashing light streaked across the heavens, and when I gasped, Eliza spotted the fireball, too. A brilliant light flaming the Western sky, with a tail curved as a horseshoe. We cried out, and our whole band stood gaping in awe as the sky put on her light show while the dogs howled like wolves.

Like all the stars were falling to Earth.

Mama says she's never seen such a sky show! Mr. Ryder thinks this has to rival "The Night the Stars Fell," which he's heard tell of from others who've traveled the same trail.

Jem says we got our fireworks after all.

Later still

Long after the fires died out, I peeked outside the tent flap and looked across the wagon circle to see one other candle burning besides my own. Mr. St. Clair's. In the tent glow, I imagined him hard at work on a drawing well past midnight.

I wish I could see what keeps him up tonight.

July 5

Stuck here at Pawnee Fork. One month since we left Independence! Mr. Ryder says we may be held up a week or more at this spot. We're waiting on some soldiers to join us, and we'll team up with more wagons headed our way.

Night

Such a funny thing has happened, though if Jem tells, I will be in sore trouble. Eliza and I were to fill the water buckets for morning, but we were so taken with our game of landing rocks in the bucket that we forgot until night fell. We thought the easiest way to avoid a scolding was to slip down to the river without notice. We had just started back, pails dripping, when we heard a noise. A scratching and a rustling. How we did cling to each other, visions of Pawnees in mind.

Then we did lay eyes on our Pawnee. Was Jem!

And so with a great rustling of underbrush and crashing of pails, we rushed at him through the dark. Then came the banging of water buckets and flying of heels! Followed by Jem's bloodcurdling yells, "Pawnees are coming! Pawnees are coming!" Jem screamed all the way back to camp.

Eliza and I and our water pails stole silently back to the wagons. What a good laugh we had to ourselves, till our bellies quite hurt.

July 6

We have some two hundred loose horses traveling with us, led by a white stallion that belongs to Captain Elias. Just today I heard the herders talking, saying they mean to guard the horses doubly well tonight.

Later I awoke in the middle of the night to hear the white stallion screaming, Jem heard it, too. Mules running and braying. We were both too afraid to go outside. Then something struck our tent, and the whole thing collapsed on top of us. Darkness and mayhem all!

Mr. Ryder yelled at us to get into the wagon.

By morning, we discovered the whole of our two hundred horses were missing. Disappeared!

Captain Elias is sure of it being Indians, but Mr. Ryder says, "Who can say? There are horses thieves about these parts in every direction." Still, he advises us to have eyes in the back of our heads.

July 7 (Fourth day at Pawnee Fork)

I've collected bunches of watercress, which I planted in some soil in a broken dish. Every day I'll give it a little bit of water, and watch it grow. We'll have fresh greens to eat long after we've left the river behind.

I went to seek out the artist to show him the sketch I've finally finished of Mr. B. Never have I seen a more striking picture than the one Mr. St. Clair has painted today. He's made a buffalo hunt a thing of beauty. All light and shadow, with colors gold as prairie grass that seem to come from the sun itself. I saw the thrust of the Indian's spear in his serious face and the tense muscles of the horse in pursuit and I feel as if I've been there myself, staring into the whites of the buffalo's eye.

After seeing the painting, I could not bear to show him my feeble sketch of Mr. Biscuit. I attempted to hide the page beneath my apron, but Mr. St. Clair spied it, anyhow.

He took one look at my sketch and told me I am an artist!

Later

After supper I thought to see about my watercress, only to discover it gone! I fear a rabbit has eaten my little garden already — unless that rabbit be named Mr. Biscuit.

July 8

Today Eliza and I made our acquaintance with a tarantula. The hairiest, scariest *araña* in the world! Our chore was to gather buffalo chips for building a cook fire. Eliza reminded me to kick them first with my boot. Underneath live spiders and many legged centipedes, not to mention scorpions.

I was kicking at them and filling my skirt when we heard Jem stomping on the ground behind us, chanting. "Tarantula! Tarantula! Come out! Come out! Tell me what it's all about!" I thought he was just being silly, when sure enough there appeared a giant spider, walking on legs like stilts! Before I could satisfy my curiosity, Jem stomped the poor thing with his boot. I yelled at Jem that the spider wasn't hurting anybody. Yet part of me couldn't help thinking I would not want to meet such a hairy creature in my bed tonight.

I shiver just thinking of it.

July 9

180 miles till we reach Bent's Fort.

Louisa is good with words. She entertains me with riddles while I sketch in my book. Here are some, to which I have made a picture for the answer, and we shall have ourselves a riddle book:

Threads of seven colors are stretched on the great prairie.
(rainbow)

Ten flat stones we each carry with us. What are they?
  (*fingernails!*)
Runs through the valleys clapping its hands.
  (*creek*)
Has little shoes of dirt. Whistles night and day.
  I guessed Jem! But the answer is (*grass.*)

I have made up my own riddle for Louisa:
What is the color of harvest-moon gold, a treasure to
hold?
  (*honey!*)

  I told Louisa she must share some of Aunt Florence's
honey with me, since she has guessed the riddle.
What guilty pleasure!

Middle of night

Such a knot is there in my throat and a tightness
in my chest, I can hardly bear to write what has
happened.

  Jem woke in the night to screams, and shook me
awake. They seemed to be coming from the other side
of our wagon circle. Mama and Mr. Ryder heard them,
too, and we ran outside to find the Nuttings fully

awake next door to us. Across the circle of wagons, a most horrific sight caught my eye. Flames glittering against the black night, long after the campfires had been put to bed.

The artist! It seems he must've fallen asleep and somehow tipped over his lantern and soon his tent went up in flames, taking Mr. St. Clair along with it.

To think that just hours ago I fell to sleep most peacefully, and dreamed I was sleeping on a feather bed, with roses the color of fire in my hair.

My heart's broke.

Mr. St. Clair's death, a stone in me.

Can't bear to write another word.

July 10

Heaviness in the air. Our whole company shrouded in gloom. Hands can't seem to move. I'll never take up a pencil to sketch again.

Louisa has come with news of Mr. St. Clair's sketches having burned up along with him!

Our loss is unthinkable. Such sorrow, unbearable.

The men already prepare the grave. I wish I were a tortoise with a shell to crawl inside of. I can't bear to think of oxen stamping over his grave, as if to erase where the artist has been.

later

WE LEAVE PAWNEE FORK.

I'm writing with the artist's thick pencil. That and the sketch of the Indian dance are all that is left of him.

Doesn't feel right to leave this place without Mr. St. Clair.

Like leaving Papa's grave back in Arrow Rock.

Camp No. 26

Traveled only six miles today.

More wagons with us now, 75 or so filled with goods — 150 in all, which slows us down a good bit. No matter. I am in no hurry to be far away from Mr. St. Clair.

July 11. Camp No. 27. Coon Creek

Mama was taken sick tonight, with pains she can't account for. She's taken some medicine given her by

Mrs. Nutting, but Dr. Antoine has gone ahead with the companies before us, on to Bent's Fork. I sit here writing when I should be saying extra prayers for Mama. I wish I had a book to read to her. I must confess, I miss books more than baths.

July 12

Wednesday morning.

Mama shows no signs of improvement. Mr. Ryder has in mind to ride ahead himself to see if Dr. Antoine, the Frenchman from St. Louis, can be stopped.

All we can do is wait, wait, WAIT.

July 13

Mr. Ryder has returned to say Dr. Antoine could not be caught. He assured Mama we'll head direct for the fort, where the good doctor will be detained. The doctor, we are told, is most skilled in midwifery.

Mr. Ryder was all gentleness and affection on his return, telling Mama we should thank God that the Frenchman knows especially about female cases. But the fort is still eight or nine days journey, and already the blush is drained from Mama's face. Mr. Ryder frowns, and on his brow are two half-moons of worry.

July 14. The Caches

Noon rest. Stopped twenty miles this side of the crossing, where we visited a train of large holes dug in the ground, in the shape of jugs, to my way of thinking. Frenchie says they are called the Caches (sounds like *kash-ez*), from a French word. A man rumored to have escaped from prison made them! Near as I can tell, the man goes by the name of Beard, and was overtaken by a severe winter storm. I imagine him a pirate, direct from Robinson Crusoe, which Jem begs me to tell each night around the fire, since we had to leave the book behind. This Beard fellow lined the holes with moss, sticks, and stones to conceal his goods until he could return for them. On his way back to recover his store, he was attacked by Pawnee.

Jem and I could not help wondering what stolen treasure was kept hidden there! Eliza said, "Just think what gold and rubies could have lain in this very hole." Louisa remarked that I can now embroider a treasure chest for one of my quilt blocks.

While the four of us entertained visions of stolen jewels and finery, Mama has been weeping. When Jem and I returned, her eyes were puffy and her nose red as Indian paintbrush.

Mama seldom cries.

Camp No. 31

Went to bed by eight and a quarter o'clock, but sleep did not descend long. I awoke to lightning flashing jagged tongues in all directions. Thunder followed, and rain poured. Not a spoken word could be heard. The tent shook and loosened the pegs from the sand beneath us until the whole shelter was likely to collapse with the tempest. I was most fearsome that something terrible would come of it.

Mr. Ryder attempted to carry Mama to the wagon, but the ropes from the tent tangled somehow, and in the confusion the pole fell on her!

Mr. Ryder would not let us in directly to see her.

Mama was soaked through and through. Mrs. Nutting brought dry blankets to her aid. I do not see why Mrs. Nutting should be allowed entrance and not her own daughter!

July 16

Today Mama sat up, smiled weakly and called the mishap a "shipwreck on land." It promises to thunder again tonight. Pah! I told Jem, "I hope we have no more shipwrecks."

"Except for Robinson Crusoe," said Jem.

July 17

Today marks the midpoint of our journey to Santa Fe. Halfway to our new home. We have come over four hundred miles and have been on the trail six weeks!

Tomorrow we reach Cimarron Crossing. It sounds to Jem like cinnamon, and he's sure we will find cinnamon candy growing on trees. I told Jem, "Now I will never smell cinnamon without thinking of Louisa and Eliza," for I just found out this is where I shall have to say good-bye to my dear friends.

The trail splits here — there's been much debate over the two routes. Mr. Ryder insists that we take the

Mountain Branch, and I confess to being most anxious to see some snowcapped peaks rather than being parched in a desert. He says he must do some trading at Bent's Fort, but I can tell he's worried over Mama, and needs to get her to a safe resting place for a few days.

The Nuttings and many of the others who've joined us will take the Cimarron Cutoff, which they say is one hundred miles shorter. But crossing the Arkansas at Cimarron Crossing is highly dangerous. After that, it's sixty long miles with little water until the next river. Word is people die of thirst in the Cimarron Desert. And the traders say the Kiowa and Comanche are sure to attack on that route. What if Louisa and Eliza should be attacked by Indians? Drown in the river? Die of thirst?

Noon rest

I overheard Mama tell Mr. Ryder she thinks herself well enough to take the Cimarron route! My heart leaped like a pond frog!

Then I heard Mr. Ryder say back that the desert route is called La Jornada Del Muerto, the journey of death! He says water is so scarce and so many traders

die of thirst that they often have to notch their
horses' ears and drink the blood to stay alive.

I solemnly do not want to be parted from my
dear friends, but neither do I wish to drink horses'
blood!

July 18, morning

The time has come.

I must say good-bye to my friends. I'll leave them
each with a gift, besides the cottonwood seeds bound
for California. For Eliza, my drawing of Mr. Biscuit,
so she can always remember her hero. And for Louisa,
four patches of cloth sewn into a small cover, each of
which I have embroidered with her favorite wildflowers so that she will at least have something to wrap
round her violin.

I have asked Louisa and Eliza to sign their names
here in my diary, just like Aunt Florence's autograph
book, the one with the red velvet cover, which she
had us all sign before leaving home.

Cows like pumpkins
Calves like squash
I like you,
I do, by Gosh
    Eliza

I thought, I thought,
I thought in vain,
And so at last
I sign my name.
    Louisa Nutting

Eliza has given me a silky hair ribbon to keep, which she says she won't wear, anyway! What a funny girl. I use it now to mark the page in my diary. Louisa has written me a song and played it for me on her violin! I can't recount the words here without crying buckets.

Later

Good-bye, farewell, *adiós* seems all this journey is about. Louisa and Eliza are gone. Seems to take forever to find a true friend, but only a moment to lose one. And I have lost not one or even two, but three!

It takes a full day to cross that river. What if Louisa and Eliza did not even make the river crossing? What if I should never hear from them again?

Camp No. 34

I am lonely and have fallen under the cloud of my own bad weather.

Camp No. 35

Mosquitoes. Thunderstorm.

Camp No. 36

Saw my first snowcapped mountain far away in the distance. Mr. Ryder says it must be eighty miles or more. They call it Pikes Peak, or James Peak. I should like to climb a mountain someday, but have not the will for it at present.

Later

Have been humming Louisa's song. Here is what I remember of the words:

Over the trail
Under the moon
Across the sand
I'll think of you

Camp No. 37

Mama is doing poorly.

July 22

Came upon some traders camped here, who've said we are but fifteen miles from the fort. Mr. Ryder seems to know them as old friends. One Mr. Cooper is said to be a rich man, but I can't see it. And Mr. Fayette is quite a beau. Mama found him quite charming, though she commented, "Where he'll find a bride in these parts, I can't imagine." Jem, like a mosquito, would not leave Mr. Cooper alone. He dogged him with questions of California and gold until I had to yank him away under pretense of washing before supper.

July 23

We passed a soldier's encampment — fifty or more tents in a ring with soldiers drying clothes in the sun! One might think there's a war on with so many soldiers, but I don't believe we'd find them at their washing, were it so.

One had a scar across his eye and looked like a statue standing guard until he marched up with his musket to ask, "Where you goin'?" My heart beat most furiously, but I thought Jem's eyes might come clean out of his head. The soldier said to Jem, "Go ahead, touch it. It ain't no snake," pointing to his scar. "Got me this in the Mexican War."

Jem declined the offer, but the soldier did let us pass without delay once we gave him our destination.

Camp No. 39

In sight of the fort!

July 24. Bent's Fort and a roof!

The fort is like a castle built of mud bricks, which Mr. Ryder says are Mexican *adobes* baked in the sun. The walls are six feet thick to make it safe from fire on the inside. Over the main gate is a watchtower with a belfry. I long to hear a bell sounding again.

There is only one door and, inside, a space as large as a palace! I feel I am indeed a princess of the Plains.

Twenty-five or more rooms surround the open space. One is a dining room, another the *cocina*, a kitchen, where I hear the cook singing. A blacksmith shop, a store with real goods to buy, a barber, and an icehouse, perhaps more exciting than the store! I shall be content to chew on ice for the whole of my dinner.

I've been inside the trade room. There are things there from all over the World! Tea from China, bells from Germany, clay pipes from England, glass beads from Venice, wine from France, and guns from Pennsylvania.

The blacksmith was most friendly to me, a furry man by the name of Mr. Vieth. His shop is most mysterious of all — it has the feel of night even in the day — dark, glowing with redhot coals and ringing with metal. A giant bellows hangs from the ceiling, giving air to stir up his fire. He makes horseshoes and door latches and handles — there is nothing that man can't make or fix by bending and twisting metals as if they were strings of licorice.

*   *   *

Mama says this is a rough place, and I don't think she's referring to the coarse furniture. All I can think is how long it's been since I felt a roof over my head! Oh to wash at a basin again! Glorious!

They have a well here, with fine water anytime we want! There are tables with buckets on them which we are free to drink from. I have actually seen one man throw water from the bucket on the floor, as if it were nothing!

Mama says the floors have to be watered on purpose every morning to keep the dust down. I, for one, am no stranger to dust!

Upstairs

At last I find myself in a hotel, the one Mr. Ryder described. Our room is on the second story, with two real windows! One looks out on the plain, the other looks down over the yard, which they call the patio.

We have our own furniture!! I need double exclamations to say that we have a table, chairs, beds, and washbasin(!!), and we eat in our own room. This fits my idea of a castle for a princess, indeed!

If only Louisa and Eliza could share the wonder.

The ceilings are made of logs. Mr. Ryder says they're cottonwood, and I can't help but wonder if they still contain spirits. Must ask Frenchie how this works.

Jem tells me they have a billiard room up here! I'm afraid Mama will remove us at once if she hears tell of gambling. She would rather we contend with wolves and starvation and Indians than cheap morals. Thankfully she's already taken to her bed.

Jem was delighted to inform me that no girls dare enter the billiard room. We'll see about that!

Later

The doctor is here, and he's attending to Mama now. Mr. Ryder says he should be able to give her some medicine which will improve her condition. Jem and I are to go take a walk up the river.

July 25, next morning

I wandered into the kitchen, where I met the cook, and she has given me bread.

Bread oh bread. To have bread again! The world could end tonight.

The cook's name is Letty and she is a round, dark-skinned person with a great wide smile, the friendliest person I've met at the fort so far. She asked me if I'd like to see the root cellar and help her carry up some turnips, so I followed her into a small underground room beneath the kitchen. It was quiet there, so pleasantly quiet, and Letty gave me the peaceful feeling that no talking was needed. The cool air wrapped round me like a lady's silky shawl, and I told Letty I thought it must be the kindest spot between Missouri and New Mexico.

Back in the kitchen, I watched her scrape some green mold from the bacon. She reached a finger to her lips and said, "Shh! Don't tell. Our secret." I wanted to say we've seen a lot worse than moldy bacon on the trail, but I get the feeling there are some folks here who are fancy-like and just might not cotton to the thought of eating spoiled food.

I did then work up the courage to ask her if she told fortunes. She said, "Now, honey, what on earth gave you that idea? The only future I can see is what's for tonight's supper." She laughed so hard, it made me laugh, too.

Letty is famous for her pumpkin pies. She says her best pie eater is Manuel, called Manny, a boy my age who helps his father break horses in the corral.

Cook says I may help her to bake pies, and I told her, "We shall see who can eat more pumpkin pie, this Manny or my own self."

Afternoon scene

The fort is its own small city — a welcomed change from the prairie. Everywhere there's hustle-bustle and no end to new sights and new words I'm hearing. The men are gambling away the very shirts on their backs, then coming to Mr. Ryder for advances on their wages.

The plaza is filled with the clanging of the black-smith, the mountain men in their buckskins down from the Rocky Mountains, Mexican traders offering *chiles,* pine nuts, and exotic spices, and Indian hunters with buffalo robes by the hundreds. Even soldiers milling about looking so serious!

It is like a symphony just to stroll through the place. So far I do believe I've heard seven different languages. Cheyenne, Comanche, French, Sioux, Spanish, Ute, and my own English. And dare I say the mountain men have a language all their own!

One such colorful character they call Muldoon. A regular Kit Carson! He wears a flaming red shirt and leggings made of buckskin. He says he does his own sewing of clothes, but who ever heard of a man sewing? (Mr. Ryder should take some lessons!)

Anyhoo (as I heard this Muldoon say!), he walks about on slippered feet carrying a flintlock musket, and everywhere hanging from him is beadwork of one kind or another — his knife case, tobacco pouch, flint and steel, etc., which he makes himself. I thought it just another tall tale until I saw him with my own eyes, all squinty-eyed catching beads on his needle. He has tiny round glasses, and a red beard that nearly reaches his waist!

Wheresoever he goes, he leads around a one-eyed mule named Reuben, and the funniest thing about Reuben is . . . that mule wears a *sombrero* — complete with feather!

I immediately felt shy of Muldoon, so I couldn't look him in the eye, but I did so want to pet Reuben . . . I made myself go near him, and Muldoon called a friendly "Howdy do, miss!" to me. He right away began telling me he was back from a rendezvous in the mountains, which I took to mean a big meeting place where traders gather and have more fun and games than they do trading. He said, "Rendezvous this season was the best doin's ever! Got me three skunk tails for my hat and up and won Reuben in a tomahawk-throwing contest! A bigger fool never drew breath than the one parted with Reuben."

Evening

Dr. Antoine has given Mama some medicine and some advice: to rest. She's not to get out of her bed, or stray far from her room. Mama says the advice is much easier to swallow than the medicine!

We're all glad of the rest, and feel safer knowing there's a doctor at hand. I think Mr. Ryder has drunk one too many toasts to Mama's good health this eve. He growls loud as a bear, and laughs too hard at his own jokes.

July 26

Today is my *cumpleaños* — (thirteenth) birthday! I had not imagined it passing without notice, but Mama complains of feeling strangely — her back, head, and hips — and I do not wish to bother her. When she tries to get up out of bed she holds her hand over her eyes like she might faint.

*   *   *

Seeing as how it's my Bustin' Out Day (according to Muldoon), he promised to teach me how to shoot a musket. What would Mama say? I begged Jem not to breathe a word of it. I am not one for killing things, but I sure would not mind shooting me a dried-up old cow chip!

We walked out back to the meadow, and he showed me where the powder goes and about the tiny patch of cloth that catches the spark so the musket can go off. Then he showed me how to load it with a genuine musket ball!

Shooting is much harder than I thought. I aimed at the cow chip, but the gun went off so loud, it near made me jump my skin and I fell backwards. A few more times I got to shoot off his musket, and Muldoon said, "Afore you know it, you'll be fit for the girls' shootin' match up to Rendezvous."

I knew he was just blowing wind, but I liked his kindness all the same. My shooting, for all its noise and racket, didn't go anywhere near that cow chip!

He wants me to try again tomorrow, but I figure I best count my chickens and put an end to my shooting days before Mama catches wind of it.

July 27. morning

There's a small woman with bent shoulders and sad eyes who helps Letty in the kitchen. I've noticed her hair hanging in her face and the fact that she doesn't like to look at a person when you speak to her.

Letty has told me that some Pawnee killed her husband and captured her, and she's so sad on account of she had a seven-year-old son and doesn't know what happened to him. One late night after she was captive in the Indian camp, she crawled right out of camp on her belly and stole a pony! She rode it all the way back without saddle or bridle until she found the trail. Some traders picked her up on the way and brought her here, where Mr. Bent gave her some work and some hope, too. He said if her son be alive, surely some traders would pick up word of it. But she's been waiting two years and no word!

Letty showed me how to roll out the dough just right. And how to cleverly flip it upside down into the pan using my whole arm. We made up a baker's dozen of pies at one time! She says the key to her pie is extra ginger. All the while we were rolling dough, I worked up my courage to ask Letty how she came to the fort.

Now if I understand her correct, she says she was a

slave somewhere else, I think Missouri, and so was her husband. She told me how he was so brave in helping Mr. Bent in an uprising in Taos, that Mr. Bent himself somehow freed the both of them. I don't understand quite how this could happen to Letty or how Mr. Bent got her free, but I'm sure and certain glad he did. Letty said to me, "You wouldn't think it, child, but pie-making goes faster with storytelling." I'm guessing we each have our own stories, some with happy endings, some not.

Soon the pies were ready, and we used long-handled paddles like boat oars to slide them into the *adobe* ovens out back of the kitchen. But not without scorching every hair off my arms, and my eyebrows, too!

Noon

Have gobbled down three pieces of pie in place of noonday supper, but I'm afraid Manny (not to mention Jem) has outdone me, and all on top of supper, too.

With our bellies too full to move, we plopped ourselves on the *banco* (bench), and I asked Manny some Spanish words. The Mexican traders speak so fast, they're hard to understand, but Manny's good at teaching! We looked around the fort and he pointed to things, then slow-ly pronounced the Spanish word. In just minutes I learned *cinco* new words. *Sala* is large room; *candela* is candle (easy to remember!); *caballo*, horse; *pájaro* means bird; and I won't forget *empanada de calabaza* (pumpkin pie)! He also taught me sayings like, *Vaya con Dios* (Go with God) and *¡Silencio!* (which I've already used on Jem several times).

Then he pointed to us. *"Dos amigos,"* he said. I knew without asking.

Two friends.

later

Jem came back from the river with Manny all out of breath and screaming Great Jumping Grasshoppers! I guessed from his ghost-white face he'd just seen a band of Pawnee. So I gingerly stepped outside the gate and looked, but did not see any Indians. I heard only a loud buzzing sound, like a swarm of bees had gotten right inside my head.

That's when I saw them.

Hundreds of them, thousands. Millions! Jem was righter than right.

Grasshoppers!

Those glassy-winged creatures covered the walls of

the fort until you could not see a speck of *adobe*. A wall of grasshoppers! If Mama could come downstairs to see them, I'm sure she'd say a Bible plague had descended on us.

All the grasshoppers in Kansas Territory must be paying us a visit. Manny shut the gates to keep them out, but they still crawl into the folds of my dress, burrow in my hair, and land in my soup!

Jem and I have taken to exclaiming Great Jumping Grasshoppers at the slightest thing! Manny and Jem have started a game. We each catch a grasshopper and call, "Spit tobacco! Spit tobacco!" and sure enough an unsightly brown liquid issues forth from those creatures!

July 28. Bent's Fort. morning

There's all manner of wonders in this place. I poked my head into the parlor this morning, where I'm sure I was not supposed to be. A woman sat combing her hair all the while not withstanding the presence of Mr. William Bent himself. I knew it had to be him because he had a fancy shirt with a stand-up collar, and a scarf tied round his neck that looked like silk. He sat speaking with another man who may have been a captain or colonel or even a general! Beside the woman stood a crock of grease, which she applied so generously, it dripped like rain from her hair. Never before have I seen a lady washing her head in grease!

Mr. Bent laughed when he saw me staring. "Women will rinse their hair in anything to make it shine," he told me. He said his own wife, Owl Woman, rinses her hair with a tea made of mint.

Jem'll never believe I met Mr. Bent himself and he was talking to me about ladies' hair, of all things!

Night

I am un-lonesome, with so much to see and do here! Every evening is occasion to celebrate — greeting new visitors as if each one is President Polk himself! Always there's dancing. Letty is the best dancer of all. She kicks up her heels and flounces her skirts as if she were a schoolgirl my own age. I could not help but think of Louisa Nutting — how her violin playing would add to the celebration.

Manny dragged me into a round of Cuna, their cradle dance (not for babies!), which I don't know in the least. So I just held on and followed along. I felt more like a grasshopper than a dancer, compared with

Manny. The dance is like the waltz, where you stretch your arms out to form the sides of a cradle, except the whole room started spinning as Manny swirled me around until I was dizzy as a doorknob.

Later Mr. Vieth let us have some of his tallow candles for a race. These candles burn fast, so Manny and I each lit one, then watched to see whose would go out first. The winner is the one whose candle lasts the longest. I am sorry to report mine did wink out first, so Manny got his wish, which was for one more (grasshopper) dance!

Long after Jem and I go to sleep, we can hear the men carousing — so much drinking and gambling goes on here, it causes new furrows in Mama's forehead.

July 29

Jem and I heard a most strange cry coming from the belfry. What do you think we found but two caged-up bald eagles perched right atop the bell! A caged-up bird is sadder to me than a fish out of water, so we flipped the latch and there was such a tornado of wings, it nearly caused a wind to knock us over!

Just as Jem and I were congratulating ourselves on our good deed, we heard the men in the plaza pointing and shouting. We thought it just another row until Mr. Ryder came and made us "acknowledge the corn," as in tell the truth.

When all was said and done, Mr. Ryder was quite disturbed with us. That freedom flight will cost him two horses! It seems the birds belong to another trader who was to be paid two horses in exchange for their feathers!

This trading business is hard to figure. How a few feathers could be worth a horse is beyond me!

Mr. Wendell has said the Cheyenne are skilled at capturing these birds, and brought two of them here to trade. Mr. Wendell talks like a book and has lived at the fort for some time. He knows the ways of the Cheyenne. Mr. Ryder says he speaks their language better than any Anglo in this whole entire country.

July 30, mid-afternoon

What yarns the men spin! I can't any more tell false from true. The men squat half the day on the dirt floor around a pan of dried meat. They smoke clay pipes. These pipes start out as long as my arm, but day by day they break off pieces and throw them on the ground until the pipes are quite short and I can't help but fear they'll set their hairy faces on fire!

One called Old Bozeman struts around like he's the biggest toad in the puddle. When he leaned over to light his pipe, his wig fell off and he was balder than a bald eagle. Jem and I now call him Old Baldman.

Old Baldman tells one where he killed himself eleven grizzly bears. The hairy man next to him brags that he once lost an ear wrestling a mountain lion. Of course Jem has every one of those stories stuck to memory.

Later, Jem asked me if all those stories the traders tell in the plaza are true. I told Jem I think most of it's just plain bragging. A lot of hoorah, if you ask me. But Jem is full of questions, as usual. "What about all those strange things they say about Indians?" he asked me.

Now this surprised me coming from Jem, who was always one to believe the worst when it came to Indians. I myself am torn on the subject. So I asked him what the men were saying.

Jem said they talked of how the Cheyenne raided a Kiowa camp and stole a little white girl that was only two years old. Or one time when a woman left her husband, he raised his baby on buffalo milk. And there was one where a Ree shot his own son straight through with arrows, then plastered him up with mud and brought him right back to life.

I told Jem one thing I do know is, there's plenty of white folks who feel unkindly to Indians of any kind.

I'm not sure if I told him the right thing or not. It's hard telling good from bad out here. Right from wrong used to be a whole lot easier back in Missouri. But I'm sure glad to know there's something in that head of my brother's besides rocks!

Later

Jem said he saw a white man giving sacks of grain to a Cheyenne woman. The bags were right heavy, and the man wasn't helping her carry them. So Jem went over to see if he could help and just as he came upon her, she dropped the bag and it split wide open. And what should come tumbling out? Not corn or grain. Rocks! That bad egg was cheating her blind, filling the bottoms of his sacks with rocks just to cheat her out of some grain.

I hope they toss him in the *calabozo* and he has to stay a long time in jail.

After supper

Just this night, Letty was telling me how Mr. Bent himself owes his life to the Cheyenne. Apparently he had been ill almost to dying, where he could neither swallow nor speak. His wife, Owl Woman (called Mis-stan-stur by her own Cheyenne), forced a hollow quill down his throat and was feeding him broth she blew right from her own mouth, the way a bird might feed its babies.

When Owl Woman saw he wasn't getting any better, she called on a famous Cheyenne medicine man. He took one of Letty's big spoons and held down Mr. Bent's tongue. Now this part makes no sense, so I asked Letty to repeat it twice. She did indeed say sandbur. He rammed a bunch of these thorny burs down Mr. Bent's throat, and when he pulled them up one by one with a thread he had attached, they pulled out with them all the stuff that was sticking there making him sick. When the so-called operation was over, Mr. Bent sat up and swallowed soup on the spot.

How I wish that medicine man could work his magic on Mama. She sleeps most days and complains of the pains as soon as she tries to sit up or stand. Letty says the Cheyenne brew a tea from wild cherry bark that cures most ills, and I aim to find out how to get me some for Mama. But first I have to find something worth trading for it.

July 31

A white wolf kept coming around the fort this morning at daybreak. The men all thought it was a dog since it didn't look like the other wolves, so they lured the dog inside with a bait of raw meat and slammed the gate shut behind so's the other wolves couldn't get in. Soon the nice doggie went plumb crazy and chased near every person in the fort up onto the roofs. The men from up on the roof finally managed to lasso it, and they put it in chains and locked it in the bastion. All day it stayed there snarling and howling and growling bare-fanged at any human to come near.

But then Muldoon came and strolled right up to that lunging, snarling creature and patted its head, of all things! I swear that Muldoon could tie down a bobcat with a piece of string if he had the mind. From now on, that wolf is Muldoon's critter that follows him everywhere, kind of like Reuben.

Night

Tonight we had the most fun — a taffy pull! Letty boiled up a batch of New Orleans molasses and added to it sugar and butter and lemon and even vinegar (which thankfully you can't taste). As soon as the sticky mixture had cooled off, Letty handed us each a portion for pulling.

I pulled and pulled and pulled, and we were laughing and making it a contest. Manny was showing me how to pull just the right amount, then how to shape it into something. I pulled mine into a thin rope light as honey, then braided it together until it looked like a fancy horse's mane. Manny formed his initials, M R, out of taffy, for Manuel Rodriguez. Then I added an F before the M R, forming my own initials! When Letty was not looking we threw some at each other, and Manny got pieces of it stuck all through my hair!

Poor Jem started too soon and now has blisters on his skin! He ran to get some water and by the time he got back, his taffy had cooled off and was sitting there, one big ugly toad of a lump. He had no problem eating it, anyway.

August 1

There is a funny old goat here they call Agnes, and Jem and I have seen it running up and down the ladder leading to the roof!

Midday

Nothing to do, so Mr. Ryder started a game where Jem and I keep count of the birds we have seen here. I am doing my best to sketch each one, and Jem says we should make them into a bird book for Mr. Ryder. So far we have seen:

turkey vulture (ugly)
Mississippi kite
red-tailed hawk
bald eagle (in the belfry, of course)
golden eagle (huge)
hummingbird (doesn't hum but is fast)
killdeer
kingbird (attacks everything)
magpie
turtledove (sad sounding)
redheaded woodpecker (reminds me of Muldoon)

blue jays (everywhere — I like to save their feathers) and a burrowing owl, seen in the middle of daylight!

In the middle of our bird hunt out back of the fort, a Cheyenne girl came up to us on her pony. She wore a buckskin dress that had been tanned to the color of honey and looked soft as silk, with fringes on the bottom and beads and red cloth. The right side hung longer than the left. Underneath, she wore leggings made of the same. Her long hair hung down her back in two braids, shiny black as a raven's wing. I am afraid to say I could not keep my eyes from staring until I saw Jem gaping at her like he was seeing a ghost.

She let us pet her pony and then she showed us a trick her pony can do. The girl let out a high-pitched whistle, and the pony lifted its head and whinnied, showing great teeth that made the animal look like it was laughing at something awful funny. Then with a hand signal she got the pony to stop. Jem tried to ask her how she did it, but before we could figure out how to say it in a way that she might understand, she hopped into her saddle and was gone like a bird.

Next time I shall take an apple with me, for the pony.

August 2 (tenth day at the fort)

I went outside the fort again today, in back of the corral, to search for Indian trade beads. They're called white hearts because they're rimmed in red glass on the outside with a white heart of glass at the center.

While digging around in the dirt I was keeping a watchful eye. I was sort of hoping for a new friend on account of missing Louisa and Eliza. Caroline, too. No sign of the Cheyenne girl or her pony. So I sat in the dust and ate the just-in-case apple myself, letting the juice run down my arms.

Later, Muldoon came up and told me he wanted to make me a real, honest-to-goodness bona fide trade. He held out a pouch he had beaded with an hourglass shape of blue beads and white beads all around it. Inside was a piece of flint and a steel for making fires.

I could not think what I could trade that would be worth one quarter as much. That's when Muldoon said all I had to do was make him some pemmican.

Pemmican! I thought for sure and certain he had to be talking balderdash. But he wasn't. Pemmican is a most foul-tasting concoction that Muldoon calls dessert. Letty taught me how to make it, with lard, berries, and jerked meat, but it comes out tasting worse than buffalo chips!

As smart as Muldoon is, I'm the one who'll make out like a bandit on this trade!

August 3

This morning I had just gathered a small handful of red beads when the Cheyenne girl happened upon me. She jumped down from her pony and knelt in the dust with me to gaze at my beads. When she saw the few dusty beads I'd collected, she laughed like she had just heard a most funny joke. She pointed to her own white beads, then the blue beads she was wearing, letting me know that these are more prized than red beads!

Then she appeared to ask me a question. *"Netones evehe? Netones evehe?"* she repeated. I finally began to realize she was asking to know my name. I'm afraid I said "Florrie, Florrie," much too loud. Then, realizing we had no difficulty *hearing* each other, but rather, understanding, I myself had to laugh.

I pointed to a flower, the closest thing I could think of to my name, and she said, "Vehpotse!" Her eyes lit up as if she had just found a long-lost friend, and she now calls me Vehpotse!

Then I asked her name in return, and she pointed to a black-headed bird with a long tail and said, "*Mo'e'ha,*" then pointed to herself and repeated, "*Mo'e'ha.*" She then let out a series of *ee* sounds just like the bird itself. Wait till I tell Mr. Ryder of her skill at birdcalls.

I didn't guess her name was Bird, so I asked Mr. Wendell at the fort and he did say Mo'e'ha sounds like magpie.

Of course! My new friend's name means magpie.

later

After studying the magpies, I have made a serious sketch in my diary. This bird has a black beak and head, intelligent eyes, white wing patches, and a tail longer than its body. The tail has some of the shiny colors of Mr. Bent's peacocks at the fort. This puts me in mind of Mr. St. Clair and his paints. How I wish he were still with us in this world. I'm sure he would happily lend me some color for the magpie's tail.

I suppose I may never make sketches without thinking of him in sorrow. Would that I could show him this drawing — I've become a real student of nature and think this one of my best. But I'll have to ask Jem, who never fails to tell me the real and honest truth!

August 4

The days I see Mo'e'ha pass much faster than the ones where I wait for her but she doesn't come. Most of the time we wave our hands in the air trying to tell each other something, then laughing at our own efforts. Sometimes we draw pictures with a stick in the dust to show what we mean. If she draws one moon, or folds her hands and closes her eyes to show she is sleeping, I know she means that I will see her after one more sleep. Tomorrow.

August 5

Today I learned some new words.

mo'eh no'ha = horse
o ne a vo kist = beads
wo pe she o nun = blanket

And *hah ko ta* means grasshopper. I told Jem and he has been chasing grasshoppers all day, yelling, *"hah ko ta"* with glee when he catches one.

Mo'e'ha laughs her bright laugh, a sound clearer to me than water. The new sounds of her language feel strange and sticky on my tongue. I know I must sound terribly silly, but I think it pleases my friend to see me try to learn. When Mo'e'ha says Florrie, it sounds like two notes of Louisa's violin music. I wish I could close my eyes and ask her to say my name over and over. When she says *horse,* that is a different story! She says *or-sa* with a low growl in her throat, which I think just might scare her pony away!

Night

I've heard Mama cry out in the night from the next room. I struggle to know how I can be of help to her. Sometimes all I can think of is to take her a cool cloth for her forehead. Some small comfort.

August 6 *(two weeks at the fort)*

I did not go to see Mo'e'ha today but instead read to Mama from a book I borrowed from Mr. Wendell called *Two Years Before the Mast*. It tells the exciting adventures of a Mr. Richard Henry Dana, who sailed the seas on a clipper ship from Boston to California. She was kind to mention several times how good it made her feel, and remarked on how a good story takes a person's mind off her troubles.

I think she dozed and missed a most exciting part, when he rounds the Horn and nearly hits a reef in a terrific storm. When she wakes, I'll recount it for her in my own words, complete with sound effects.

I have noticed that Jem listens from outside the doorway while he whittles, hanging on to nearly every word. Then he runs off to tell Manny the story.

Jem is whittling a spoon out of cottonwood for the baby. I have told him it will be some long time before the baby can eat with a spoon, but a wonderful present it is still.

August 7

Mama is worse.

August 8, morning

I heard Dr. Antoine telling Mr. Ryder that Mama's fever is not coming down, and he fears for the baby. Even Dr. Antoine seems at a loss.

This has given me an idea, for which I need Mo'e'ha's help.

Late morning

Mo'e'ha said yes, and I am to meet her this very night. At our rock.

Late, before bed

It is deep night with scarcely a moon, yet Mo'e'ha moved silently as an owl and did not seem to stumble as I did at every rock or root or stop cold to peer into the darkness or startle at the sound of a snapped twig. How I envy her surefooted moccasins! My own boots have become so slick-bottomed from wear that I can hardly keep a foothold on anything these days.

She led me to her village. Fires lit the night air, and sparks everywhere rose like stars to the heavens. The Cheyenne village is made of cone-shaped lodges in a circle by a stream. Even in the flicker light I could see that each one was painted green and red and black with animals and figures and symbols. Feathers fluttered like flags, buffalo tails hung from poles, and strings of little hoofs clicked in the wind making a most musical sound. In front of each lodge was a lance, shield, or medicine bag that announces who lives there.

Mo'e'ha led me to the doorway of what seemed to be her home. *"Nahko'eehe,"* she said to me, pointing inside the lodge. Then she held a hand up like she does with her pony and motioned for me to wait in the shadows.

All I could hear was a raucous barking of dogs. They seemed to announce my presence to the whole village. For the first time I felt a chill race up my spine, aware I was an intruder. I smelled something pungent, a mixture of leaves and sweet grass burning and sage that tickled my nose. I waited. I tried not to think about what I was doing. I tried not to think about my pounding heart. I thought only of the herbs I needed for Mama.

In the darkness I heard the Cheyenne chanting and singing their evening song. I closed my eyes, letting the sounds run through me like rain, and it calmed my beating heart.

I took with me a gift in exchange for the tea. Honey. From Aunt Florence's jar. But as I stood waiting outside the lodge, I began to worry that honey, though precious to me, seemed such a small thing. Should I have brought coffee and sugar as well?

Soon Mo'e'ha came out of the lodge and with her a tall woman with raven hair like Mo'e'ha. Vermilion shone on her cheeks and from the part of her hair. "*Nah ko ee he*," my friend said once again. I could only think that perhaps she meant *my mama*.

The beautiful woman handed me a small bag, and I reached inside the pocket of my apron to give her the honey. She smiled and nodded her head, and I thought she seemed pleased, though she waved me away as if I should hurry on my way.

A bit of honey seemed small thanks, and my words even smaller, so I was left to hope that my face had given thanks enough.

August 9

I have boiled some wild cherry bark tea for Mama, but not without a scolding from Letty. Does she have eyes in the back of her head to know how I came by the tea? I have even added some of Aunt Florence's precious honey from the wagon, to sweeten the mixture and give Mama a drop of home.

late night

Mama awoke with the severest of pains, relieved only by some of the cherry bark tea and medicines given by Dr. Antoine. The pains, which lasted well until midnight, had us all fearing that the baby was coming, and too soon.

Then Jem and I heard a cry, and we hugged each other with joy, for we thought it to mean the baby had arrived safely! But soon we were to discover the cry was not our own sister at all, but another baby girl birthed this very night by an Indian woman in the room just below. It hardly seems fair — one family's sorrow is another's joy tonight.

later still

The worst has happened. Mama has indeed birthed the baby before its time. The wee thing was too small to live. All hopes for having a sister are crushed! Mama sunk into Mr. Ryder's arms and, though she is in the next room, she appears far away.

The baby, my dear wee sister, is dead.

There. I said it.

August 10, morning (day 18 at the fort)

I feel immovable. Like the blacksmith's metal turned cold.

I lie and stare at the ceiling. Even the cracks in the mud wall take on the shape of a broken heart.

Late morning

I am filled with so much anger and hurt that I took my quilt to Letty and asked her to burn it in the fire.

Letty fixed me a cup of boiled milk with cinnamon and nutmeg. It didn't seem right that anything taste so good to me. Letty insists on saving the quilt for me in case I feel differently when the sorrow has passed. I protested, but she said, "Florrie, honey, you know what they say? Only a fool argues with a skunk, a mule, or a cook." So I let it go.

Can time really mend this sorrow?

Suffering and sorrow, that's what this trail's made of.

Later still

Mama has named the baby Missouri. When she first said it aloud, it almost sounded like Misery. The name Missouri fits fine with all things left behind. Mr. Ryder dug a small grave behind the fort, and Jem nailed up a cross for the baby's burying place. We made a marker that said,

HERE LIES MISSOURI RYDER
BORN AND DIED AUGUST 9, 1848

Sad evening

The four of us stood by that tiny grave holding hands and bowing heads and whispering prayers. Father Morgan, the priest who prayed with Mama when we first arrived at the fort, came to say some sacred words over the grave. And I picked some prairie flowers to set here.

Bedtime

I feel a scream growing inside me, a scream so loud, it could pass through these thick mud walls so that Mr.

Bent himself might awaken. Mr. Ryder has instructed me to leave with him the day after tomorrow morning. We will leave Mama here. I'm mad as a horned toad!

I don't want to leave Mama when she's still unwell. And I don't want to leave the fort, either. To think, I will never see Mo'e'ha or Manny again!

According to Mr. Ryder, we must continue on to Santa Fe. We will head for the Raton Pass, and there will be no water until we reach the Purgatoire River. I feel as if I am in Purgatory already!

My job is to cook and take care of Jem. Jem already fancies himself a man — let him go kill a bear. He never minds me, anyway, and as for cooking, Jem says my salt-rising bread makes for good doorstops.

If I have my way, Jem and Mr. Ryder shall soon be eating grasshoppers. Boiled.

Mr. Ryder says it's my duty and I mustn't grouse. So I am GROUSING TO YOU, Diary, where Mr. R will never know.

I tried pleading my case with Mama, but she lights her candles and says the Good Lord has no attachment to people or place. I can't help but wonder if the Good Lord knows anyone like me!

In two days' time, Mr. Ryder, Jem, and I shall be dodging wild bear and mountain lions.

How I could howl with the coyotes tonight!

August 11 (day 19)

When I saw Mo'e'ha today, I quickly drew a picture in the dust. I drew the fort, and our wagon, showing her that we must leave. In two sleeps. We collected berries in silence for a short time, then she mounted her pony and rode off without a wave.

August 12 (day 20)

My last day before we leave the fort. I wait and wait for Mo'e'ha, but I never hear the clicking of her pony or see a flash of black hair through the trees.

She does not come.

A little while later

I waited what felt like half the morning. Still no sign of Mo'e'ha. Mr. Wendell once told me there's no word for good-bye in her language.

August 13, good-bye to Bent's Fort

My heart was heavy at not seeing my friend one last time. I went down to the rock, our rock, where we'd met so many times.

A pair of moccasins! They were soft as a newly shorn sheep and had a flower stitched on the front of each one — a flower, like my name, stitched in red beads. Whitehearts! The beads I'd admired so much.

A gift from Mo'e'ha.

I cast about looking for some sign of her. I thought I heard the soft snort of her pony, saw a flash of raven hair. I must have imagined it. Or did I?

Then I hit on an idea. I unlaced my old boots, the boots that had walked me many a mile but were now too slick for use. I slipped on the moccasins, which fit as snug as a hand in a glove. The shoes I left on the rock, not as a gift, but as a weight to hold in place the drawing of the magpie, ripped from my book.

I hoped it would say without words that I loved the gift of moccasins, and that I think of her. Mo'e'ha. Magpie.

Later

All in a hub-bub getting ready to move again.

Before leaving, I carved FLORRIE with Jem's knife in the wooden rim of the blacksmith's bellows. That had me grinning, thinking who might discover it first — Manny or Mr. Vieth. Manny helped us load the wagon and bid us *"Vaya con Dios"* at least three times. Muldoon called, "Hey-o! Florrie! Keep your chin to the wind!"

Hardest of all was leaving Mama. She hugged me a good-bye, and I spilled tears on her clean dress. She said she'll join us soon, soon as she's stronger. I try to believe her.

I can't imagine what's ahead without Mama.

We spent a few more minutes hugging and wiping our tears and listening to Mama's reassurances, Mr. Ryder all the while acting fidgety. The few extra minutes so long to him were a blink to me.

It breaks my heart leaving Mama here to her sorrow.

Mama cautioned me, "Don't look back," but I couldn't help myself. I squinted in the sunlight at the earthen castle, Bent's Fort, growing smaller and smaller in the distance.

Jem and I may never return to this spot.
Baby Missouri will never leave it.

Six miles out

How strange to be back on the trail. Feels as if we're
beginning all over again when we've been nearly three
months out!

Came six miles up the river, and we leave it behind
us now. Crossing the Arkansas feels as if we are truly
entering a foreign country.

Mama made me promise I'd make an effort to look
on the bright side. But I miss my friends from the fort
already. I'm weary, collecting memories like beads
with no string. Too much leaving.

Jem seemed sad for Mama when we first left, but already he's acting like we didn't just bury a baby sister.
I don't know whatever became of the spoon he
started. Haven't seen him whittle in a while. He seems
to think only of guns. What a mystery boys are! He's
happy as a pig in mud to be back on the trail. Forever
singing, which annoys me into secretly cursing that
everlasting tongue of his. In between singing, he's
taken up spitting.

August 14

Made eighteen miles today. No longer plains, as much as sand hills. "Green" is not a word they know here. Breakfast was a bowl of dust!

Jem and I have seen the mirages. False ponds, indeed. We're so thirsty, we keep seeing water glittering plain as a church on Sunday, but then we get to it and find it vanished.

Mr. Ryder's given us an explanation, which he read in Josiah Gregg's book. He calls it "refraction" — a fancy word for saying that the sky appears to be below the horizon. I have my own word for it.

Cruel.

Gets the heart seeing things it can't have.

August 15

Mountains! Two of them appear in the distance. One is known as Sierra de la Madre and the other Sierra Grande. Mr. Ryder says we are indeed seeing what they call the great Rocky Mountains.

No water. Stopped at a difficult pass in an *arroyo*. Waiting for Frenchie and the wagons to catch up.

Some of the men were talking about gold, a magic word to Jem. His ears perked like a rabbit in a field of hawks. They were telling about how Mr. Bent picked himself up some real gold nuggets on his way from Jim Bridger's fort out to Wyoming. One man was saying gold was around here, closer than California. I had to check to make sure Jem's eyes were still in his head.

Another man told us the story of the gold bullets. Seems there was a Southern Cheyenne they called Chief Whirlwind. He led a war party that had only three guns, and they ran out of bullets. They found some yellow-looking dust on the ground and worked it into balls for musket shot. Later, they defeated a band of Pawnee — the story goes every one of those yellow bullets hit an enemy.

Golden bullets! What will they tell of next?

August 16. Hole in the Rock

I've not seen it with my own eyes, but it's said there's a rock at this place filled with the coldest, clearest water to rival Big John's Spring, and a bottom has never as yet been found. Jem says, "Even a bottomless well could not meet his thirst." I agree.

Frenchie presented me with two fine hares, which is quite a treat since I won't eat the antelope killed by our baggage wagon and am nearly ravenous enough to eat a bear myself.

August 17

Stuck here at Hole in the Rock and can't move. Our cattle ran away during the night. Several men have been searching for them all the day. Mr. Ryder does not care to go on without them. I for one do not wish to pull the wagons ourselves!

Could not have picked a prettier spot to wait.

Jem and I have taken a walk in some piñon woods and collected the nut of these pines. Each nut is smaller than a kidney bean and has a sweet crunch. We filled our bellies and our pockets. I thought to myself that we went "nutting," but the joke would be lost on Jem. Missed Eliza and Louisa all the more.

Beneath the trees we found balls of sticky sap the size of a hen's egg. Frenchie says it's turpentine, and can be used to rub into sore muscles. Just in time — sore muscles are ahead in these mountains!

Just now discovered thirty-nine of the cattle some sixteen miles from camp.

August 18. Purgatoire River

Traveled twenty-five miles or more! Held over at the camp of last night, waiting while wagons are repaired. A daily occurrence now.

A slight rain helps keep us from choking on dust. First drop in over three weeks. Makes the world smell new!

Dampened a rag with rainwater. I am dead set on having a bath. No easy task with so many men about. Thankfully, I have Mr. Biscuit to keep a lookout.

Some call this the River of Lost Souls. Jem asked one of the Mexican traders why it's so called. Old Juan said, "There's everywhere stories in these parts, and this one goes that a long, long time ago, a tribe of Comanches were so cruel, they got forced by the Great Spirit to live underground. Their punishment was to never again see the light of day. So the story goes."

Jem says he heard moaning and groaning along the riverbank just this morning. I heard it, too. Old Juan just says, "It's like them mirages. Everybody sees 'em, but can't never find 'em."

August 19. Raton Pass

Just beginning our difficult trek through the mountains. Mr. Ryder says the Raton is the steepest stretch
of the trail. My back's telling me he's right. Oh, the
constant jolting! And it goes on for twenty-seven
miles! Never have I seen such a rocky road!

Happily, our tent is now atop a high hill. Jem has
his heart set on seeing a bear. Or a panther. Even a
mountain lion. Just the thought of it makes me stick
ever closer to Mr. Biscuit.

August 20. Wagon Mound

Mountains! All around us. Feel small against the great-
ness. One rock towers above the rest. Jem named it
Wagon Mound — it looks just like the top of our own
covered wagon!

Our wagon turned over this morning. The mountains may be full of beauty, but they're in no way kind
to wagons. Every few feet are large rocks and steep
hillocks, just the things to bounce a wagon to break-
ing. I walk and walk. I change from brown to browner
as the dust clings to me, then blows off, then sticks
again.

Beside each stream I look for some curiosity ...
a shell, a pebble, an unusual flower, the quill of a
new bird. Keeps my mind off the up, down, up,
down.

August 21

Still the Raton. Half a mile an hour. *El camino* (the
road) worse and worse.

Turkey, prairie chickens, and hare abound. I'm be-
coming quite the cook. Letty would be proud. Jem,
on the other hand, gets out of greasing axles and other
chores on account of his broken arm, which should be
healed up by now, if you ask me.

Later

Seen a bear! Not a live one, but a carcass in the road.
Now I think I see them everywhere about. I cried out,
but by the time the others came running, my bear
turned out to be an ox!

Worse and worse the road.
Each *crash* makes me think a wagon's gone over the

precipice and tumbled into pieces at the bottom of the canyon.

Only six or eight hundred yards today! The wagons snap at every turn. We lay up to repair yet another broken tongue. I have to hold my own tongue — does no good getting my temper in a flare.

August 25. Rio Colorado

Out of the Raton at last! Has it been only five days there? Seems forever.

Jem's disappointed we leave without seeing *un oso*. An alive bear, that is. Dead bears are fine with me.

Crossed Red River

Put me in mind of Ash Creek and I was not anxious to enter it, so I climbed up onto a tree stump. Mr. Ryder lifted me up onto his horse, and before I knew it I was landed this side of the Rio Colorado.

Mr. Ryder has been more than kind to me (Jem, too) since leaving the fort.

August 27, Poni Creek

Hailstorm. My shawl is not thick, and two blankets are scarcely enough at night. I've taken to reporting the weather like Mama used to do (to my annoyance), but it keeps my mind straight.

We cross this stream twice. First on stepping stones by foot, then on horseback, to avoid the deeper places. Mr. Ryder has gone to help the other wagons over crossing No. 1. The banks of the creek are extremely slippery from the rains, and he has had to double up the teams, or a wagon may be turned over. I am left in charge to choose a camping ground.

I've chosen a spot where we can tuck in from the wind. Jem showed me that the tall mountain in the distance is capped with snow like Pikes Peak. I did not believe it with my own eyes, so we used Mr. Ryder's spyglass and sure enough, we are again seeing snow in August!

Nooning at Rayada Creek

There's no rest at noon rest! Work, work, work! Day after day, only time for the cooking and the washing and looking after Jem. Haven't felt much like writing. Seem to not have the heart for drawing.

Warmer today. Coming out from under wraps like a rattler after a thunderstorm.

August 29. Ocate Creek

Hills again. Thickets of trees. Jem still on the lookout for a bear.

August 30. Ojo de Gallinas

Long, dark night. Endless. Just when it began to feel hopeless, we saw the light of campfires ahead. Mr. Ryder said, "Them fires is like a straw to a drowning man."

August 31. Mora Creek and Settlement

Nooning it at the village of the *rancheros,* the men who raise cattle, which they call *vacas.* Their houses are made of mud and are hardly bigger than a pig's sty, fenced in with nothing but sticks. They eat an ugly cheese made of thin milk and *pan de maiz,* which seems to be corn bread. They try to sell us their *pan,* a bread so hard it could nearly break a toe if dropped. Jem and I felt guilty that none of us saw fit to buy their bread, so we gave them our piñon nuts we'd been saving.

September 1. The Vegas

A most embarrassing scene is what I write tonight! We came to The Vegas, and suddenly there was a crowd of some two or three dozen children pointing and shouting and covering their mouths with laughter. I couldn't think what made such a funny curiosity when I did realize it was me! Those little ones swarmed me like bees, touching my skirts and pulling down my shawl to gaze at my hair.

Jem says it was better than a monkey show at the circus, and Mr. Ryder teased that he should have charged 15¢ a look. I guess seeing a person of white skin with dark red hair's no different from how I felt seeing my first Indian. Still, it's nerveracking to be stared at like that.

Dinner was *tortillas* made of blue corn (yes, blue!). These we used in place of knife, spoon, or fork, much to Jem's delight. There was cheese speckled over like Letty's bacon at the fort, and *chili verde*, a strong mix of meat, peppers, and onion that woke my tongue right up. Roasted corn and a fried egg ended the meal. And the best part — I, myself, did not have to cook!

I kept most quiet, unnerved by the staring eyes of even the dogs. But I did try out some of my Spanish words from Manny, and though I know I made a mess of it, everyone nodded politely just as if I were speaking plain English.

September 2. near San Miguel

I'm glad for once that Mama's not here. The women around these parts often wear nothing but a chemise and petticoat, or their *rebozo,* a scarf that acts like dress, shawl, bonnet, or apron. I'm afraid I've now done some staring of my own!

They pull their clothes up above their knees and paddle through the stream like ducks. Since Mama is not here to remind me about being unladylike, I joined them, though Mr. Ryder says I shall not go as far as smoking *cigarillos!*

Wagon broke ... AGAIN! At the little creek just the other side of San Miguel. While we waited for the repair, I spied a chaparral bird, which they call the roadrunner. Must sketch it! What a funny bird. Runs fast as greased lightning on skinny bird legs, and its tail feather longer than it! Mr. Ryder tells me it runs fifteen miles per hour! Faster than our wagon. Wish I could run fast as that bird all the way to Santa Fe.

September 3, Pecos

We actually set foot among the ruins of an ancient pueblo. How could there have been Aztec people here building a temple over five hundred years ago! There used to be a town here, a town built on a rock in the shape of a foot.

All that remains now is a giant footprint.

Mr. Ryder has told us that a race of giants, more than twice his own size, built the temple here, even before the Aztecs. I thought perhaps this was just another of the giant tales, but he claims bones have been dug here of gigantic size.

Seems there is no end to the mysteries and marvels of this place we call Earth. Oh, the red rock! Like being in a painting.

Tomorrow, Santa Fe!

Is there a happy ending for us?

September 4, outside Santa Fe

Last day out. Soon we will lay eyes on Santa Fe. I'm anxious to see if the women here also wear nothing but petticoats. The journey's made me braver than most, but not brave enough to go about without my dress on!

Jem says the best thing about New Mexico Territory is eating without knives, forks, and spoons, to say nothing of plates. He can't get enough of the blue tortillas. Sendavel says such corn as we saw in The Vegas grows blue right on the stalk. *¡Madre mía!* Blue corn!

Later

Santa Fe! Mr. Ryder said we should be proud to enter under the Star-Spangled Banner. This is America now. Jem asks, "Does that mean flags'll fly for us?" Jem would have nothing less than a parade for our welcome.

September 5, Hilltops above Santa Fe

Bells! We hear them calling *bienvenido,* welcome.
Santa Fe at last!

Just realized I've been holding my breath. The men are madly washing their faces and combing their hair before we enter town. Even Frenchie runs a comb through his surly mustache!

I myself am dreaming of a bath. A real bath!

later

We heard shouts of *"Los Americanos!"* even before we could see the town. Jem and I had imagined ourselves a city. A city with castles and turrets and towers. We passed through a great wooden gateway and found instead a set of skinny streets lined with a smattering of mud houses, bright strings of red peppers drying, and brown babies crying.

Many houses have barred windows. Jem asked Mr. Ryder, "Is this a dangerous place?" but I did not hear his reply.

Dust has kicked up everywhere, and if you ask me, the whole place smells of sweaty mules!

Our wagons wiggled and jiggled their way among donkeys, goats, and Mexican chickens running through the streets. Never have I seen so many dogs in one place. Mr. Biscuit is in doggie heaven! Doing our best not to run them over. We came then to a *plaza.* A tall man leaning on his rifle showed us where to go.

In the plaza

When Jem and I jumped down from the wagon, dogs barked at us, small children stared, and women smiled shyly from under black shawls. New Mexican and Pueblo boys chased after one another playing a stick-and-ball game in the street, while girls sat at a clapping game. Jem could not wait to join in.

There's a warm feeling about the place, something oddly familiar that makes me feel at home (except for the sweaty-mule smell!). Like mud-pie houses we built in Missouri when we were little.

Mr. Ryder had to register and pay his taxes at the customs house. The drivers line up to collect their wages. So Jem and I are alone in this place.

Without Mama, how will we ever call this home?

Later

I know Mama asked me to look on the bright side, so I'll tell you, Diary, I'm secretly happy for a place to put my feet down. Evening is setting, and the sky colors light the desert on fire. The air turns to milky blue. At last we're cooling off. Soft lights glow in taverns and dance halls, where we hear much noise and carrying-on, as well as the strumming of a *guitarra* and mandolin. I've seen La Fonda, a great mud-walled inn, not unlike a small version of Bent's Fort. I wonder if this is where we are to stay. A real hotel!

Tonight we sleep in the wagon while a place is made ready for us above Mr. Ryder's shop. In the land of traders, would that we could trade our wagon for a hotel room!!

September 6, morning in Santa Fe

Mr. Ryder introduced us to his partner, Carlos Villarreal, who runs the shop with him. Mr. Ryder's partner takes a caravan to Chihuahua, traveling the Camino Real, and brings back goods to trade like Mr. R does from Missouri. He is kind and "a most beneficial trader," no small praise coming from Mr. R.

Mr. Villarreal has a friendly face full of smile, and was nice enough to speak extra careful-like so we might understand him. On first meeting us, he said, "*Ah! Señor Ryder! La Señora es muy linda. Y que es*

major, ella es muy afabla, muy placentera, muy buena."
My face heated up red as the desert sun, knowing he
was talking about me. Then came Mr. Ryder's hearty
laugh. He kept repeating the words *hija, hija, daughter, daughter,* until I realized that this man had mistaken me for Mama. Mr. Ryder's wife!!

I would have flushed a thousand times more red
had not his wife, Lupe, come outside just then, with
her children and an old woman they call Abuelita.
Grandmother. *"¡Hola! ¿Qué pasa?"* I said. Lupe took
Jem and me in her arms as if she had known us a
thousand years. She must've known about us missing
Mama. I liked her right away.

Carlos, the oldest boy, is only Jem's age, but he
looks as tall as me. Juan is next. he's a shy one, digs his
toe in the dirt more than looks at people. He made
fast friends with Mr. Biscuit. Then there's little
Rosalita. With a laugh that makes her eyes shut tight
and sounds like the trill of a bird. She'll do just fine
for a little sister!

Mr. Ryder's shop is nearly as big as the trade room
at the fort, and just as exciting. Stacks and shelves
of baskets and kettles and pottery jars, calico cloth
enough to clothe a hundred ladies, tools and shoes
and blankets. Fancy hair combs, church-type candle-

sticks. Even playing cards and a parrot that says, *¡Buenos días!*

Jem says, "We must be rich!"

Evening

We're to sleep in a cubbyhole of a room behind the shop, which is usually the storeroom. Lupe's worked hard to make room for us. Mr. Villarreal and Lupe will take care of us and look in on us here.

On our second day here, Mr. Ryder appears to deal more in playing cards than he does in business. I'm writing while we wait for him outside the hotel. A noisy place — some are dancing the cradle, which puts me in mind of Manny, but I dare not go inside.

In a few days, as soon as he's finished with his business, Mr. Ryder will head back to the fort to fetch Mama. The trip on horseback should go much faster. He can spare but a few good men, so I fear the danger will be greater. If only he could team up with some soldiers for protection. What if something terrible should happen to Mr. Ryder on his way to the fort?

I wish he never had to leave us, but since I long to see Mama again, I tell myself to have a stout heart. Mama would wish me brave.

September 7 (day 3 in Santa Fe)

Already Mr. Ryder prepares to leave. He's taken us to a store with a candy counter! The candy was in a glass case, as if each piece were a valuable piece of jewelry.

Peppermint and wintergreen and horehound! Red-and-white-striped candy. Piles of it. Heaps of it. Mountains of it! Licorice in jet-black strings like boot laces and braids nearly as thick as Mo'e'ha's! Even in the shape of Mexican *sombreros*. Candy that looks like shelled corn and candy hearts. (Jem won't eat those!) Best of all, we found tiny dots of red candy that turn our tongues scarlet. So hot, Jem and I stick our tongues out to the wind.

Candy, glorious candy!

Lupe helped me choose something from Mr. Ryder's store to send back for Mo'e'ha. I chose a small nugget of turquoise the color of heaven. Three times I instructed Mr. Ryder on where to leave it for her. I pray he shall not forget!

September 8 (day 4)

Jem listened in on Mr. Ryder talking with Mr. Villarreal and another man, a shady-looking character with shifty eyes I've seen playing cards at La Fonda.

I'm afraid now we must both bear a terrible secret.

Mr. Ryder, it seems, has lost everything at gambling. Well, perhaps not everything, but a good deal. What will Mama say! Jem has overheard him paying the man horses and sheep, mules, blankets, and buffalo skins — near the entire load we brought from Missouri, from the sounds of it. And all was said and done in whispered tones and hushed voices. It must be a fortune, were it gold! What are we to live on?

Jem is downcast, to say the least. We've gone from rich to poor in just a few days. What if Mr. Ryder should have to give up the store? We'd have no place to live and no means to survive. What on earth will Mama say, her children poor as orphans?

Later

Not long after discovering we're in the poorhouse, what do we see but Mr. Ryder going into his shop, where he tore open a bale of calico. The women of the village near ran crazy, like Jem and me at the candy store. They came in dozens and could not get enough. Soon the whole bale of forty-five pieces was gone, and all I could see were bags of corn and flour in its place.

At least we shall not be starving! How I wish I could inform Mama that Mr. Ryder has gone completely *loco*.

Good thing he takes leave in the morning — at least he'll not be gambling away more of his hard-won fortune.

September 9

We said our good-byes to Mr. Ryder, and I found myself all choked up. Alone with Jem in this strange place! On our way back to the shop, Jem went and found a land terrapin. Poor thing was scared and drew its head back into it shell. No sooner did I turn my back than I found Jem standing barefooted on top of it! "Jem!" I called to him. "Get down, you fool! How would you like to have your back stepped on?"

I'm afraid within minutes of Mr. Ryder's leave-taking, I've already failed my duty to Jem, speaking so sharply to him.

I confess to feeling turtle-ish myself. I wish I could

crawl inside my own shell till Mr. Ryder brings us Mama.

September 12

Three days have passed. I feel lost.

Afternoon

Discovered the marketplace, my favorite part of Santa Fe so far. What a wonder! Piles and piles of foodstuffs. And the dazzling colors! Heaps of red and green peppers, blue corn and golden melons.

A young boy came over selling melons. He told me *"dos reales por una,"* which I took to mean two *reales* for one melon. Just smelling it I knew I had to have the fruit, so I bought it from him with coins Lupe gave me for helping her in the shop. Just as soon as I turned to walk away, he laughed and laughed and said to his friends, *"Tonta, tonta,"* pointing to his head.

I asked Lupe what *tonta* means, and she told me it means foolish! Then she explained that a melon should only cost one *real* and says I'd better stick to trading. How I did feel greener than a new pumpkin!

I was plenty sore over being called foolish, but then I tasted the fruit — the juiciest melon a person ever knew. I thought it well worth the 14¢!

There is so much to see. Woven rugs and embroidered shawls as colorful as the rainbow of fruits. Beaded moccasins and coats, silver trimmed saddles and spurs, Pueblo baskets and pottery jars, too many to count. Strings of prayer beads and Mexican turquoise! That stone looks to me as if they plucked a piece of sky and brought it to earth.

Pueblo women can be seen swiftly tying grasses together. One appears to make a hairbrush, another an *escoba* (a broom, which every household needs most desperately here). Even a bone collector — old buffalo bones and those of the prong-horned antelope and wild mustang. He sells them for $5 a ton!

How it all makes me dizzy!

I've spent hours drawing — a string of peppers, a wreath of flowers, a single bone. Drawing, I'm a little less lonesome.

September 13, evening

We take our meals now with Mr. Villarreal and Lupe and their family. Each meal is nearly a celebration. Jem's in heaven, eating with his hands all the time and sitting on the floor to eat whenever he wishes. After our dinner of *tortillas,* rice, beans, spicy *chile* meat, and hot soup, Abuelita tells a story.

She is called a *cuentista,* a keeper of stories. Abuelita knows many old tales from her own mama and grandmother, some funny, some frightening. Jem and I are improving our Spanish with each *cuento* she tells. Manny would be proud! We understand only half the words, but most of the meaning.

It's impossible to tell if the stories are true. But her whispered voice alone could make night fall, or cause the moon to come up.

Her stories makes me disappear. For a time.

The first night was the story of two old women who rubbed themselves with magic powder, took three steps forward and three steps back, fell into a tub of water, and changed themselves into owls!

Then it was the shepherd who was given the gift of understanding the language of the animals.

But the favorite, which Carlos and Juan ask for over and over, is the story of *La Llorona*, the Crying Woman. It reminds me of The River of Lost Souls.

We gather round Abuelita. She lights a candle and pulls an empty chair within our circle, so we each may invite a guest to hear the story. (I can feel Papa with us.)

The story goes, once there was a beautiful young woman who fell in love with a rich man's son. They had a baby, but they weren't married, so the young man's parents wanted to take the baby away from her. When she found out they were coming to steal away her baby, she ran down to the river with her child. They had dogs with them to help find her, and the dogs could be heard up and down the valley.

As they came near, she threw herself into the river. The current was so strong, it ripped the baby from her arms and though she was saved, her baby drowned.

To this day, *La Llorona* can still be heard wandering up and down the riverbank, moaning and sighing, calling out for her baby.

Abuelita said that's why she's called the Crying Woman. And that's why children should never stay out after dark, or go near the river. *La Llorona* might think you're her child and snatch you!

Abuelita says if you don't believe the story, wander down to the river and listen for yourself. You'll hear Crying Woman moaning, OOOOOOOOO! EEEEEEEEEE! OHHHHHHHHH!

The moaning sent chills up my spine . . . even though I know it's just a children's story. Poor Rosalita! Her eyes popped clean out of her head, and she chewed on the end of my apron most furiously.

As soon as it was finished, Jem broke the spell with complaints of a stomachache. Too many *tortillas*, or too many scary stories? Abuelita gave him mint leaves to chew, which seemed to help.

September 14

Lupe has in the center of her kitchen a *mola* stone, and showed me how it's used for grinding corn and making *tortillas*. What a lot of trouble, but the final outcome is ohhh so good.

First she soaks the corn till the husks fall off and tosses two handfuls into the hollow of the stone. Then she kneels and rubs the corn up and down, up and down, till it's ground into a paste finer than sand.

Now she takes a small mound of the corn paste and

pats it out into *tortillas*. Slap, slap, slap. Like the children's hand clapping game.

Next she throws a *tortilla* on the griddle, which she flips quick as a magic trick, and without burning hand or sleeve.

I was most anxious to try, only to find my back ached from the grinding within minutes. My first attempt was more mud pie. How Rosalita and I did laugh over the sticky mess stuck to my fingers. Over and over I tried till finally I formed one worthy of putting on the griddle.

Making *tortillas* is an art. I need plenty more practice. But the art of eating Lupe's *tortillas* takes no practice at all!

September 19

Little time to write . . . have been helping Lupe more and more at the General Store. She sees I'm lonesome. Often I amuse Rosalita while Lupe makes the trades, but today, I am a merchant! A real trader! A woman came to purchase a dress, but we could not agree on the price. She insisted that Mr. Ryder sold for less, but I'm sure she was mistaken. I told her if he let the calico go for two bits, he should not have. She claimed she would wait for him, or Mr. Villarreal. I held firm, stating my price of *dos y media,* for I am sure two and a half is its worth!

After all was said and done, she left with her calico after all, at two and a half!

September 23

Mama should be on her way to us by now. No word as yet.

October 15

Diary! How my heart nearly stopped when I found you missing! I thought my life had surely ended, not knowing how to go on without you. All my pressed flowers have come tumbling out, which caused me to think of Louisa and Eliza. Wondering where they are, what they're doing this very minute.

As it turns out, the rascal Jem stole my book and hid it from me. The scoundrel! Sakes alive, what a mean joke. He has me madder than a March hare. He'll get my attention now. And worse, if I find he's read a word of it.

October 20

Jem and I have learned to play a game they have here in the streets called *kanute* (they say ka-noot). It's like the shell game we played at home, where you hide something under a few nutshells, then mix them up and try to guess where the something his hiding. Only here we play it with little sticks and pinto beans. How I love to beat the others at their own game! I'm quite good at the skill of "hand is quicker than the eye." Soon I had a pile of red beads (which I have to sit on to keep from being stolen), an apron full of piñon nuts, and other trinkets.

If Mama could see me now, that would sure put a stop to my gambling days. I'm even getting a glimpse of how Mr. Ryder could lose everything.

October 21

In a fix over Jem.

His arms now stick out a mile from under his sleeves. His hair is grown near as long as mine, but he won't go near a pair of scissors and refuses to wear shoes. His skin is still dark from the sun. I envy how easily he speaks the Spanish tongue, but I'm afraid Mama won't recognize her own son.

All that boy ever wants to do is play kanute. And when he's not gambling, he's cooking up some kind of trouble. So I've had to put an end to both our gambling days and start making Jem go to the Catholic church on Sunday. It's all I can do to get him to wash his neck and ears before attending. He has no problem playing his games of ball against the church wall all the day long. But never does he think to go inside.

I took him to San Miguel, which is a church over 250 years old and beautiful. Its red earth tower, like the hand of God, points the way to Heaven, and glows red in the evening sun. A person can't but feel holy in such a place.

We listen to the prayers, same as Mama's, and I pray to God some holiness rubs off on Jem. It's been ages since I've heard Jem recite his prayer about seeing the face of God. I dutifully asked Jem to tell me one good thing about the sermon, just like Mama used to do.

His reply. "It was short."

October 22

This morning, Lupe discovered me crouched behind a barrel of corn in back of the store, crying and falling all to pieces with worry about Mr. Ryder having gambled everything away. *"Dios provida,"* she kept saying. *God will provide.* In between sobs, I told Lupe everything, in half-Spanish. She laughed out loud, and waved Mr. Villarreal over to us.

How humiliating! I thought she hadn't understood my woes at all. Then when she explained to Mr. Villarreal, he threw back his head and laughed, too! Finally, Mr. Villarreal told me the truth about Mr. Ryder.

He did not lose everything at gambling! He's arranged to buy us our own house. With a door and windows and a roof. A house for Mama to come home to! Lupe says she will take us to see it, should I not believe her!

A real house!

October 23

We've seen the house, which looks like a mud-colored mushroom, but were it a pigsty, I wouldn't care. It's ours! Ours! *Nuestra casa* (our house) sits under the shadow of *la iglesia* (the church). We have four rooms, including *la cocina* (the kitchen) and dining room, and plank ceilings. Did I mention a roof! A real roof over our heads. Forever and ever, amen.

October 24, morning

Jem and I decided: We'll sleep in the house by ourselves tonight — on the earthen floor, with only a blanket to roll up in. Jem says it'll be just like being in our tent on the trail again.

I think sometimes he misses it.

Later

Our first night in the house. I wish never to sleep anywhere else again.

October 25

We're to sprinkle the floor with water every day, and Lupe has shown us the grass matting we can put on the floor, which will please Mama greatly.

I have put Jem to work! He helped me whitewash

the inside walls of the house which goes a long way to brighten our home. How it does rub off! Jem and I are covered in white, and look to each other like ghosts of ourselves.

October 26

Today we got yards of bright-colored fabric from Mr. Ryder's store, and Lupe has shown me how to tack the cloth up on the lower part of the wall so that the white does not rub off on us.

It's beginning to look like a real house!

October 28

Lupe gave me a small statue of the Madonna and Christ Child, which I set in a niche in the snowy walls. I keep a candle burning in this small altar, praying Mama home. It's been at least a month, if I counted days correctly. Mama should've been here by now. It's got to be cold in the mountains, and getting difficult to travel.

They say it snows here — I'm too hot to believe it. Today is hot enough to peel the hide off a Gila monster. And to think, the end of October!

Jem stayed close to home today, working steady on whittling spoons again. So good to see him occupied. He aims to make a set of four, one for each of us, which he hopes to have ready when Mama returns.

Jem and I lay on the hearth with our heads in the empty fireplace — the coolest spot in the house. The breeze coming from the chimney is like finding water on the prairie.

It gave me the idea to place a pan of milk right there, to keep it cool for us. I thought nothing of it till this morning, when I heard an unusual rustling sound and tiptoed over to discover two huge rattlers in the fireplace, come for a drink of milk! Even the rattlesnakes find it warm for October.

October 29

The last of the roses mingle with the smell of red peppers drying outside the door. Mama and Mr. Ryder still not here. Jem never speaks of them.

October 31

Jem was roused by a noise and woke me in the middle of the night. Of all nights to let Mr. Biscuit stay with

Carlos and Juan! Sure enough, I heard the sound, too. Like an animal scratching at the walls of the house, a pack rat working at something. I lit a candle and the noise stopped at once.

Not long after we blew out the candle, we heard the sound again. Again, I lit the candle and looked up and down the wall where we heard the queer noise, but I couldn't see a thing.

Jem and I had been using a trunk from the storeroom for both a bench to sit on and a table to eat off of. The animal sounded like it might be right behind the trunk!

I motioned to Jem to help me slide away the trunk from the wall. As soon as we slid the trunk from its place, we found a gaping hole in the wall of the house staring at us like a giant dark eye.

Someone, or *something,* had been just outside, digging right through our wall to gain entrance to the house! Surely it had not been a thief. We had little to steal.

Jem and I pushed the trunk back at once to cover the hole. He got his rifle and sat like a soldier on guard atop the trunk while I nailed the front door shut. Then I tied our two spoons to the latch string so we'd be sure to know if anyone tried to come into the house. Jem and I sat on that trunk all night, without so much as two winks of sleep.

This morning we hardly dared step outside. Sure enough, we saw footprints — not of Indians or wild beasts, but of a large man with shoes, a barefooted man, and a burro.

Not one but two *ladrones,* intruders, thieves, digging into our house!

November 1

I now hide a small sack beneath my apron, which holds a green moss agate Jem found for me, the white-hearts from Bent's Fort, a glittery pebble from the Pecos River, and three horse hairs wrapped around a chicken feather. It is a charm to keep away evil until Mr. Ryder returns with Mama.

November 3

Still no word from Mama. Jem and I keep ourselves busy trying not to fix on river drownings and spills from wagons. Jem whittles his spoons, and me, I dream of a garden where we'll raise beans and peppers, pumpkins and squash. And our own blue corn!

I sketched out a map of the garden.

I had in mind to plant the cottonwood seeds today, but couldn't settle on a right spot. Can't help but fill with longing, wondering if Louisa and Eliza have planted theirs.

November 7

Mama, where are you?

November 8

Something's happened to Mama. I can feel it.

If only I had the fortune-teller to see the future. . . . it's been near two months and still no word. Every time a caravan arrives with traders come through the mountain pass, I beg for word of Mama, but get none. What if Mr. Ryder never made it to Mama? What if something's befallen them on the journey? Rivers. Blizzards. Falls. Drownings. It takes courage times a thousand just to keep from thinking the thoughts.

Lupe says the name Santa Fe means "holy faith." She reminds me I must have holy faith that Mama will return.

November 9

Every day now at sunset, like clockwork, I climb to the hilltop. From this height I can see the road that brought us here. The road that will bring Mama back.

Today the clouds lined up over the red hills and light fell different on the sawtooth mountains, the stunted thorn tree, the sheep on the next mesa.

In one golden moment I saw me a sunbow. I called it a sunbow because it looked just exactly like all the colors of the rainbow, but there's no rain anywhere for miles. The sky got so clear, I thought I could see the whole trail in an instant — saying good bye to Caroline and Aunt Florence giving me the honey jar, Eliza and Louisa picking flowers, Mr. St. Clair sketching buffalo, the view from the bluffs at Council Grove, shooting stars and all.

November 10

Walked home from my hilltop lookout in some despair when I neared the house and heard sounds. A screaming, a crying, a wailing. I ran toward it.

When I finally reached home, I busted through the door all in a dash. In a glance, a flash, a single second that doesn't seem real to me now, my heart took in what my eyes couldn't trust.

Mama!

"Mama!" I shouted. "Papa! I mean Mr. Ryder."

There was Mama sitting atop the old trunk, clutching a bundle in her arms. Mr. Ryder and Jem were there, too, gazing at the bundle. (*I wondered, did Mr. Ryder hear me call him Papa?*) The bundle was wrapped in my own quilt of nine blocks, the one I'd sewn for Missouri. And that bundle was squealing the living daylights out.

¡Madre mía! The bundle was a baby! And that red-faced, loud-mouth baby with a shock of brown hair on top was to be my very own sister.

"Meet Cimarron," Mama said, and she smiled with new light in her eyes.

There was so much laughing and crying and hugging and jumping up and down and carrying on, I'm sure they could've heard us all the way to Pecos.

When all calmed down a mite and the baby stopped her squealing and I believed what my eyes were seeing, Jem and I asked Mama how it could be that she'd brought us a baby sister. "Was it a miracle from God?" Jem asked, and I felt proud just for him thinking it.

"I suppose it was," Mama said. "A *milagro*. Nothing short of a miracle."

"May I hold her?" I asked Mama.

She handed me the baby, and I rocked her in my arms. "Mama? Where, I mean how, I mean what on earth happened and how did this all come about?"

"In time," said Mama. "In time. We all have our stories to tell, and there's time enough for us now, Florrie. Don't you go worrying about a thing for one more minute. You've had enough worry to fill a wagon."

While I was bouncing baby Cimarron, Mama walked all around the house, exclaiming over this and that, remarking all the while on what a home Jem and I had made, in a voice that was real warm-like. Her Missouri voice.

In all the fuss, we forgot about Mr. Biscuit till he started howling like the wolves for some attention. Jem and I both were so filled with questions to ask and things to say, it's a wonder any of us heard a word of how we came to have Baby Cimarron in our lives. At last we got to hear the story.

Just as Mama was thanking God for seeing them through the Raton Pass, they'd stopped to rest at an area called Cimarron before pushing on to cross Ocate Creek. I couldn't hear the word "Cimarron" without thinking of Jem and his cinnamon candy trees. This all put me in mind of Louisa and Eliza back at Cimarron Crossing, and I couldn't help wishing them here, seeing this baby and hearing the story right along side me.

Mama was remarking that *Cimarron* is a Spanish word for wild or unbroken. Mr. Ryder said it was most likely named for all the wild horses and untamed sheep you see roaming in those parts. As they were sitting having their boiled coffee and some hardtack, Mama heard a sound issuing from the reeds growing near the creek, and thought an animal had gotten itself hurt.

Mr. Ryder took up his gun, and they went to have a look, and that's when Mama saw the baby all alone. Just floating there in the reeds without any clothes on, all skinny and hungry and scratched-up like, as if she'd sailed down the creek and got stuck in the reeds.

The baby was crying all the time, sick as could be with stomach upset and terrible thirst. Her tiny hands and feet were near blue in color. Mama soaked them in warm water. Every day Mama gave her spearmint and chamomile tea with camphor and castor oil, and a mustard poultice over her stomach, and all the while they worried it was the cholera. The men scouted the area for days, looking for the baby's family, but found no one. Mama and Mr. Ryder waited, for neither could bear to leave a helpless baby behind. At the same time, they did not want to take her from her rightful parents.

After a week or more of waiting, Mama became more and more attached to the baby. But so did she fear for my own well-being and Jem's, and felt a terrible need to push on to Santa Fe. Round about that time, one of the men in Mr. Ryder's party found the bodies of a man, a woman, and two boy children. Not a one of them could understand what in the world a lone family was doing there. It looked like the cholera or some such had taken them, and next to the mother there appeared to be a basket with a blanket for holding a baby.

Mr. Ryder and the men were then delayed giving the family a proper burial, even though it be a grave with no names.

Mama felt for sure and certain it had to be God's will, her finding the baby after losing her own, and that wee thing without a family. She saw it as a sign, a gift from God, a chance to give that baby a hope in this world.

On account of where they found her, and because she was a wild thing, they named her Cimarron.

Unbroken.

I look at those sweet fat hands and those teeny perfect toes and think there's nothing broke about her. It's all new, and she has the world up ahead of her in this land of enchantment. Land of Tomorrow.

November 11

Mama has brought me a bottle of perfume! A lovely blue glass bottle with a holder at the top that looks crystal-like. I am happier with the bottle than I am with the perfume inside. But most of all I'm happy Mama sees me as grown-up enough to have my own perfume, called The Rose of Youth.

So taken with my perfume that I didn't get to see what Mama had for Jem. Must ask him. Jem was most eager to present his spoons to Mama and Mr. Ryder. Mama cried at the sight of them, and Mr. Ryder said The Four Spoons would make a perfect name for this house, to be carved in wood over the door.

Then we all did remember it will have to be The Five Spoons.

Mr. Ryder has brought me an even bigger surprise — an abalone shell from Mo'e'ha! And . . . my own bed, soft and warm and made of feathers! "Nothing too good for my oldest daughter," he did say with a knowing look.

November 12

I know where to plant the cottonwood seeds now. Outside the window, where Cimarron sleeps. One day it will grow up to wave hands of fairy green at her.

November 17

One whole entire week has passed in a blink.

Today I stepped on a burr, which hurt something fierce, so I went down to the stream to dangle my feet in the water. I was staring at the same ten toes I've always had, but I couldn't help thinking of where all they'd been and the things they'd made it through. Aunt Florence was right: The trail may be over, but I *am* on a path different from whence I started.

Evening

Ate with Jem's spoons at supper tonight. We dipped our spoons way down into the honey jar and savored the very last of Aunt F's honey. Everybody agreed the end is sweetest.

Just when it seemed we must be all out of stories, we started recounting ones we'd already heard. Telling tales takes us back to the Missouri town with the scar in the rock we came from, or ahead to dreaming on the future.

Hopes for the future for Florrie M. Ryder:

Go to school
Finish quilt with three patches for Santa Fe (Five
    Spoons, the church, and a cottonwood tree)
Receive letter from the Nuttings
Teach baby Cimarron names of flowers and birds
Climb a mountain someday
See that Jem does not eat all my licorice strings

End of November

We're a real family now. Like a bone that's been broken and mended back stronger than ever. It's not like the place in us for Papa and baby Missouri is gone. It's just we're making room for the ones we have left to love on this earth.

Every night now I sing Cimarron to sleep with a New Mexican lullaby that I have heard Lupe sing to Rosalita:

Sleep my beautiful baby
Sleep my grain of gold

I often sip tea and read to Mama, and when I feel warm and sleepy inside, I crawl under a thick quilt, thinking my thoughts by the light of the moon. I'm surrounded by my own drawings, and Mr. St. Clair's, pinned to the wall. At last I fall to sleep on the new bed, the feather bed Mr. Ryder brought for me all the way from somewhere.

Epilogue

On August 21, 1849, Bent's Fort burned to the ground.

It wasn't long before Florrie and her family received sad word of it in Santa Fe. Florrie remembered fondly her time there, and the friends she had hoped to see again one day. She would never again see a magpie or dance the Cuna without thinking of Mo'e'ha and Manny.

In 1858, at the ripe old age of twenty-two, Florrie married a hardworking, song-loving man named Ricardo José Alma. A *ranchero* living outside of Santa Fe, he made many a trip to get supplies at the Santa Fe General Store, where they fell in love over a newly soaped-up saddle.

That same year, gold was discovered at Cherry Creek. Never forgetting Muldoon's colorful tales of the Colorado region, Florrie and her husband struck out for gold country, where Florrie would become known for being one of the first women to hike to the top of Pikes Peak.

With Ricardo, she stood at the top of that mountain and read to him from her book of Ralph Waldo Emerson's essays. *"Every promise of the soul has innumerable fulfilments."* Then and there, she and Ricardo decided to settle on a ranch in those very foothills, near present-day Colorado Springs. They went on to have five children.

Jem never did make it to California to find the end of the rainbow. His fortune led him instead to the Colorado gold fields along with Florrie, where he worked as a carpenter, hoping to strike it rich. His plans were interrupted by the outbreak of the Civil War. In 1861, he enlisted with Company A of the Second Colorado Infantry, where he was sent on a difficult winter march back to Santa Fe to defend against Confederate attack. Following in his own papa's footsteps, he worked as medic at a makeshift hospital near Pigeon's Ranch during the difficult battles of Glorieta Pass, the Gettysburg of the West. Here he met his future wife, Ellen, a Civil War laundress and nurse.

Florrie was to cross paths again with her dear friends Louisa and Eliza Nutting, whose family had settled near San Francisco, California. Eliza returned to Santa Fe as a teacher, in 1857, where she taught reading and writing at a school for girls established by Bishop Lamy and the Sisters of Loretta. There she was known for her lively storytelling. She always spun a good yarn or two while her students engaged in beadwork and sewing. She kept in her classroom a red leather autograph book where each of her students would write a verse every year. Her favorite was that of one of her brightest young students, none other than Cimarron Ryder.

One day on an outing to Denver, Florrie happened to pass by the local concert hall, where a playbill unexpectedly caught her eye. Louisa Nutting Edwards! That night, she attended a violin concert, given by her long-ago friend. Though Louisa now had a shiny new Hopf violin in a case lined with silk, she still wrapped around her beloved instrument an old patchwork given to her by Florrie as a parting gift at Cimarron Crossing.

After her children were grown, Florrie published a book of her sketches called *Scenes from the Santa Fe Trail*, dedicated to Mr. St. Clair. She died at her home in Colorado Springs at the age of seventy.

Life in America
in 1848

Historical Note

In the 1800s, Americans were moving west. The Oregon Trail, the Mormon Trail, the California Trail — all carried emigrants and adventurers across mud-red trails and rocky dust-gray roads through harsh conditions to new lands, new homes, new fortunes, new lives.

The Santa Fe Trail was different. Primarily a trade route, it saw few emigrant families and settlers, and even fewer women. Rather, it carried traders — wagon caravans loaded with goods for sale and barter, following the "immense highway" first blazed by the hooves of a million thundering buffalo.

Traders, eager to fetch high prices for their goods, headed for Santa Fe. However, the Mexican Territory was under Spanish rule, and they didn't look kindly on outsiders, often jailing American traders.

In 1821, as Missouri became a state and Mexico won its independence from Spain, William Becknell and four companions loaded trade items onto the backs of a few pack animals, and headed for Santa Fe.

They quickly sold everything and brought back not only bags jangling with coins, but word from the new governor that American traders were now welcome in Mexican territory.

Becknell returned to Santa Fe that same year with $3,000 worth of trade goods piled into heavy wagons. He blazed a shortcut trail, the Cimarron Cutoff, saving one hundred miles and avoiding steep mountain passes. Despite the difficult journey, including a long, waterless stretch of desert, he made it, along with a 2,000 percent profit!

Soon American traders, mostly men, began setting off from Arrow Rock, and pouring into Santa Fe. Their wagons, pulled by mules or oxen, were overloaded with fabrics, ladies' dress patterns, buttons, buckles, and all kinds of clothing and household goods. By 1827, steamboats brought St. Louis goods all the way up the Missouri River to Independence, Missouri. Here the wagons loaded up, taking nearly two months to make the eight hundred-mile journey.

Often wagons would set off in groups for safety, and at Council Grove they might join with additional wagon trains, forming circles to keep livestock safely inside. Travelers faced countless dangers: blazing heat, thirst, hunger, thunderstorms, lightning, disease, prairie fires, buffalo stampedes, Indian attacks, rattlesnakes, swarms of mosquitoes, and hazardous river crossings, to name a few.

By the mid-1840s, only a few American women had traveled the Santa Fe Trail.

In 1846, Susan Magoffin, age eighteen, pregnant, and a new bride, set out from Missouri with her husband, Samuel Magoffin, a trader in charge of a large wagon train. One of the earliest women to travel the trail, Susan fed animals and picked berries, cooked meals, sewed, wrote in her diary, and made notes of all the wildflowers, animals, and sights along the way to Santa Fe.

Her trip was historically significant for a number of reasons, not the least of which is that her journal provided an accurate daily record of trail life and happenings, from a woman's point of view. She chronicles the food, dress, habits, routine, and social customs of an ordinary day on the trail, as well as the meeting of cultures at Bent's Fort and provides a record of Santa Fe trade in its heyday, a detailing of Mexican and Cheyenne life and customs, and an account of the Mexican War.

As recorded by Magoffin, Bent's Old Fort was a welcomed sight along the Mountain Branch of the Santa Fe Trail. It stood at the crossroads, a lively trading post where Indians, mountain men, fur trappers, and traders alike gathered to trade goods and stories. Many sought to rest livestock, repair wagons, gamble, sing, dance, or fill their bellies. Like a small, bustling city with adobe walls, it contained a trade room, council room, kitchen, blacksmith shop, living quarters, as well as a billiard room, a belfry that housed two eagles, and an assortment of pet peacocks.

Cheyenne, Arapaho, Comanche, Kiowa, Apache, Sioux, and Pawnee frequented the fort to trade. The Bents were known as the fairest traders around. They built the fort on lands of the Southern Cheyennes and worked diligently to keep good relationships with the Native Americans, even encouraging rival groups to keep the peace, which was always better for business.

Peace did not reign forever, though. In 1847, one of the Bent brothers, Charles, was murdered in an uprising in Taos. A few years later, another partner, Ceran St. Vrain, withdrew his support. Cholera swept the plains and killed half of the Southern Cheyennes. Bent's Fort, so famed for its trade with the Indians, could no longer support itself. In 1849, the fort was blown up under mysterious circumstances.

Despite the demise of Bent's Old Fort, trade continued to flourish on the Santa Fe Trail, and New Mexico soon became a U.S. territory. This opened up the region to even more traders, and travel along the Santa Fe Trail increased quickly. By the 1850s, many American traders were settling in New Mexico. This meant the trail began to see more women, along with families and children.

In addition to the wives of traders, merchants, missionaries, and a few families on their way to California, the trail also saw nuns traveling southwest, the wives of military officers, and — the largest group of women to brave the Santa Fe Trail as far as Bent's Fort — were those accompanying gold seekers who rushed to the Pikes Peak region of Colorado in 1858 and 1859.

Travel along the trail peaked in 1866. That year alone, upward of five thousand wagons made the trek west from Missouri. The trail was now dotted with army forts to protect traders and transport army supplies. It also served as a mail route and stagecoach line. Alive as it was, its demise was quick to follow, with railroads having reached Kansas by 1867. Traders began to ride the rails as far as they could go, closer and closer to Santa Fe. In February 1880, the first train rolled into Santa Fe, which marked not only the closing of a trail but the end of an era. A few grass-filled ruts, poking up through patches of prairie after these many years, still tell the story.

Travelers on the Santa Fe Trail stop along the way to eat lunch and mend broken wagons.

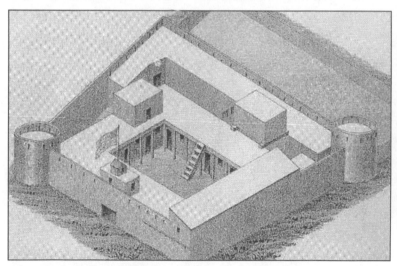

Bent's Fort stood at the crossroads of the Santa Fe Trail. A trading post for trappers, mountain men, Native Americans, and traders, travelers along the trail stopped for supplies, food, rest, and wagon repairs.

As Bent's Fort was built on Cheyenne land, Cheyenne people frequented the fort to trade, work, and visit. The Cheyenne, originally part of the Algonquin nation, were hunters and fishers in North Dakota. Fighting with other Native American peoples, however, led to their migration westward, until they settled in Colorado.

Its large size and its proximity to the edge of the Great Plains made Pikes Peak the first major landmark of wagon trains passing into the mountainous part of the Santa Fe Trail.

Traders who followed the Santa Fe Trail are greeted by La Fonda, an inn located in Santa Fe's central plaza, where the trail ends.

The Catholic Church of San Miguel, built in the early 1600s, is the oldest church in Santa Fe, and, some say, in the entire United States.

Native Americans, New Mexicans, and businessmen who came to Santa Fe from back East mingle in the town's central plaza, shopping and bartering.

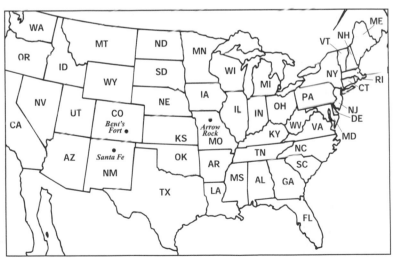

Map of the United States, showing Arrow Rock, Missouri; Bent's Fort; and Santa Fe, New Mexico.

About the Author

When I was in college, I dreamed of spending a summer in the Rocky Mountains, so I got myself a job as a park ranger for the National Park Service. When I stepped off the train in Colorado, however, I found myself in the desert, not the mountains: Bent's Old Fort National Historic Site in La Junta, Colorado.

Stepping foot inside this adobe castle began my love of history. With the ringing of the blacksmith's hammer, the smell of adobe bricks baking in the sun, and bright strings of red peppers hanging from the cottonwood rafters, I was immediately transported to another time, another culture, and a completely different way of life.

I spent the summer engaged in living history at the fort. My on-the-job training was to build a fire using only flint and steel, eat tripe stew and drink out of a tin cup, fire a flintlock musket, and sleep out under the stars, wrapped in a buffalo hide.

At the fort, I impersonated Charlotte Green, the fort's cook, where I learned how to make tortillas and johnnycakes, jerk meat for pemmican, roast coffee beans in a skillet, and bake Charlotte's famous pumpkin pies in an adobe oven.

It was here that I first came across Susan Magoffin's diary of her remarkable journey as one of the first women to traverse the Santa Fe Trail. I have never forgotten her story. This, and a notebook I kept of my own "first-hand" experiences and observations at the fort, inspired Florrie's diary, right down to the tallow candle races and the sifting of dirt and dust in search of whitehearts, those precious red beads with the white centers.

Megan McDonald is the author of the acclaimed *Beezy* books, the *Judy Moody* stories and *Shadows in the Glasshouse*. She lives with her husband in Sebastopol, California, with two dogs, two adopted horses, and fifteen wild turkeys that like to hang out on their back porch.

Acknowledgments

Many, many thanks go to historian (and sister) Melissa McDonald; expert librarian and reader Carol Edwards; Mary Ellen Grant of Olathe, Kansas; Bent's Old Fort National Historic Site in La Junta, Colorado; the Santa Fe Trail Center, Larned, Kansas; Nancy Brown at the Center for Southwest Research, Zimmerman Library, Albuquerque, New Mexico; the Kansas State Historical Society; the Governor Bent House and Museum, Taos, New Mexico; the Kit Carson Home and Museum, Taos, New Mexico. I'm also indebted to historian Marc Simmons's seminal research on women of the Santa Fe Trail.

Grateful acknowledgment is made for permission to reprint the following:

Cover Portrait: *At the Start of the Day,* by Adolphe William Bouguereau, Courtesy of Christie's London © Christie's Images/SuperStock.
Cover Background: Culver Pictures.
Page 182 (top): Travelers on the Santa Fe Trail, SuperStock.
Page 182 (bottom): Bent's Fort, courtesy of Richard Frajola, Ranchos de Taos, New Mexico.
Page 183 (top): Cheyenne men, Smithsonian (B. A. E.), courtesy of the Kansas State Historical Society, Topeka.
Page 183 (bottom): Pikes Peak, Courtesy of the Kansas State Historical Society, Topeka.
Page 184 (top): La Fonda, *Street View in Santa Fe, New Mexico,* sketched by Theodore R. Davis, Courtesy of North Wind Pictures.
Page 184 (bottom): The Church of San Miguel, Corbis.
Page 185 (top): The Central Plaza in Santa Fe, North Wind Picture Archives.
Page 185 (bottom): Map by Heather Saunders.

Other Dear America and My Name Is America
Books about Heading West

Across the Wide and Lonesome Prairie
The Oregon Trail Diary of Hattie Campbell
by Kristiana Gregory

The Great Railroad Race
The Diary of Libby West
by Kristiana Gregory

West to a Land of Plenty
The Diary of Teresa Angelino Viscardi
by Jim Murphy

Seeds of Hope
The Gold Rush Diary of Susanna Fairchild
by Kristiana Gregory

The Journal of Douglas Allen Deeds
The Donner Party Expedition
by Rodman Philbrick

For Regina Shipman Haynes

While the events described and some of the characters
in this book may be based on actual historical events
and real people, Florrie Mack Ryder is a fictional character,
created by the author, and her diary and its epilogue
are works of fiction.

Library of Congress Cataloging-in-Publication Data
McDonald, Megan.
All the stars in the sky : the Santa Fe trail diary of Florrie Mack Ryder /
by Megan McDonald. — 1st ed.
p. cm. — (Dear America)
Summary: A girl's diary records the year 1848 during which she, her brother, mother,
and stepfather traveled the Santa Fe trail from Independence, Missouri, to Santa Fe.
ISBN 0-439-16963-1
1. Santa Fe National Historic Trail — Juvenile fiction. [1. Santa Fe National Historic
Trail — Fiction. 2. Frontier and pioneer life — Southwest, New — Fiction.
3. Overland journeys to the Pacific — Fiction. 4. Pioneers — Fiction. 5. Diaries.]
I. Title. II. Series.
PZ7.M1487A1 2003
[Fic] — dc21   2002044579

10 9 8 7 6 5 4 3 2   03 04 05 06 07

The display type was set in P22 Michelangelo.
The text type was set in Old Claude LP.
Book design by Sarita Kusuma
Photo research by Amla Sanghvi

Printed in the U.S.A.   23
First edition, September 2003